BLOOD MAGIC

The Good Necromancer (Book 2)

MICHAEL LA RONN

Copyright © 2021 Michael La Ronn. All rights reserved.

Published by Author Level Up LLC.

Version 4.0

Cover design by MiblArt.

Editing by BZ Hercules.

The characters and events in this book are fictitious. Any similarity to real persons, living or dead, is coincidental and not intended by the author.

No part of this book may be reproduced or used in any manner without written permission of the author except for the use of quotations in a book review.

Very special thanks to the following patrons who support the author on Patreon: Stephen Frans, Jon Howard, Michael Guishard, Beth Jackson, Megan Mong, Lynda Washington, and Etta Welk.

CHAPTER ONE

Have you ever had someone leave you a voice mail, but you didn't want to call them back, so you ignored them for as long as you could, and then they fooled you into picking up the phone by calling from an unidentified number?

That's what detectives do when they really want to talk to you.

"Mr. Broussard, it's good to finally connect. I'm in the area and I was hoping you'd be available for a meeting."

Sheeeeet....

I stood at the old green rotary phone mounted on my kitchen wall. The caller ID next to it displayed UNKNOWN CALLER. I wouldn't have normally answered, but my neighbor was supposed to be calling me from a pay phone so I could pick him up from work. I thought it was him.

I tilted my head and angled the receiver to hear the detective better. From the quiet rush of white noise behind him, he was driving.

"To whom do I owe the pleasure?" I asked, stirring my cinnamon tea. I knew damn well who it was.

"Damian Harris, STLPD, Paranormal Crimes Division," the man said.

"Ah, Mr. Harris," I said, putting on my most convincing smile. "Sorry. I get a lot of telemarketers."

"You haven't been home the last two times I stopped by," he said flatly. "And your voice mail box is full."

"What can I do for you?" I asked.

"It's best that I speak to you in person," he said. "Will you be home in about an hour?" he asked.

A pit opened up in my stomach. I glanced at my watch and grimaced. It was four o'clock. That gave me enough time to pick up Ant'ny and pick up dinner.

"I've got to run some errands," I said, "but I should back by five."

Damian paused. "You *should* be back by five or you *will* be back by five?"

"I'll be here, Mr. Harris," I said. "It would help me, though, to know—"

"As I said, I can't discuss it over the phone, Mr. Broussard. I'll see you soon," he said before hanging up.

Call me paranoid, but I try to avoid police whenever possible. If you look at my life at the big picture, filter out my necromancy, a couple of unlucky speeding tickets, and a few library fines, I'm an upstanding citizen and I prefer to keep it that way. Plus, it's not the best look in my neighborhood to be inviting police into your house. Right, wrong, or indifferent, many of us black folks are iffy with police. 'Round here, if you get a little too cozy with them, people will think you're a snitch. And you know what they say about snitches.

Was I being irrational? Probably. Abundantly cautious? You better believe it.

Heavy footsteps pounded down the stairwell into the kitchen.

"Was that Ant Man?" a voice called.

Bo, my undead servant, strode into the kitchen.

At six feet tall with a bulky frame, Bo looked like he could throw you out of a window. He was my bodyguard. He liked the job, so I kept him around. Sometimes we fought like a married couple, but it was nice to have someone in the house after being alone for seven years.

Today, he was wearing a bright purple tracksuit with a gold chain, pearl-white basketball shoes, and giant sunglasses. His bald head was polished to a high gloss, so shiny, it could have been an alternative light source.

"You dressed to go out?" I asked.

"Oh, this?" Bo asked, flipping up the collar of his tracksuit to show off. He twirled around and his nylon pants crinkled like paper. "Just a little something I picked up."

"With my money," I said, sipping my tea and staring him down. A hot blast of cinnamon helped me relax a little.

"You better tell Ant Man to hurry up," Bo said. "The rec center has cards tonight. You in, boss man?"

Nothing could keep me away from a good game of cards under normal circumstances. Along with tea, cards were my Kryptonite. Lately, me and Bo couldn't stay away from the center. Over dozens of rounds, a few cheap cigars, and deep conversation, I played cards and trash-talked my fellow neighbors down to the bottom of the night until the first rays of sunshine broke through the clouds. We were a card-slamming, fast-talking, trash-talking crew, and with my card prowess, I always managed to skim a few dozen bucks out of their pockets, which I quickly repaid with liquor and future bets. I wouldn't have minded a good game of Texas Hold 'em tonight, enough to take the edge off. But I had a civic duty, apparently.

"Can't join you tonight," I said. "I've got to talk to the police."

"What?" Bo asked, snapping his sunglasses off. "You chickened out, man. I told you not to answer that dude's calls."

"I thought it was Ant'ny," I said, shrugging.

Bo straddled a chair at the kitchen table.

"You done wimped out, Lester," he said.

"I can't avoid them forever," I said.

"Are you in cuffs?" Bo asked. "From where I'm sittin', they got nothin' on you, man. You don't gotta tell them jack."

The phone rang, and the receiver nearly shook off the hook. This time, the caller ID displayed an array of glitchy characters.

"It's probably that detective calling back," Bo said, pointing his sunglasses at me. "You better not even think about picking it up."

My black and tan German Shepherd-Labrador mix, Hazel, trotted into the room, growling. Her ears were at attention.

"What's up, Hazel?" Bo asked.

She barked at me.

"Even Hazel agrees with me," Bo said, hooking a finger at her. "Ain't that right, Hazel? Tell him, girl!"

"Quiet, Hazel," I said.

"Don't do it," Bo said.

"Will you stop?" I asked, annoyed.

Bo jumped up and pushed me aside. "If you're gonna talk to the po-po, at least let me do it."

Bo hit the receiver with a fist and it flipped into his hand.

"Wassup."

He looked at me as someone spoke to him, and his eyebrows raised.

"Maybe this is the Broussard residence, maybe it's not. Who's asking? Uh-huh...all right...Hold? Y'all called me, and you're putting *me* on hold? For who?"

He pressed the receiver against his shoulder and wrinkled up his face.

"Hey, was that detective a chick?"

Hazel barked again. I knelt to calm her, but she skittered backward, avoiding my touch.

"Detective Harris is a *he*, Bo."

Bo paused as if considering the comment. Then a voice spoke again and he slid the receiver to his ear.

"Yap. Who's this...excuse me? Naw, you better ask somebody who you talkin' to…"

Hazel ran to my kitchen window. She sprang to two feet, craning to see out, barking louder now. Must have been a squirrel.

"Hazel, be quiet," I said.

Bo puffed. "How did you know my name? Oh? Is that right? Sheeeeet..."

"Who the hell is it, Bo?" I asked. I grabbed Hazel by the collar, led her onto the porch, and shut the door. I glanced out the kitchen window, which faced the gangway between my and my neighbor's houses. I didn't see anything.

"You got a lot of damn nerve," Bo said. "If you think you can—naw, you better let me finish—Wait...what? Uh...well, all right."

Bo offered me the phone, frowning.

"It definitely ain't po-lice," he said.

I snatched the receiver and shot him a look full of daggers.

"Who is this?" I asked sharply.

"Here's the deal," a female voice said. "Your man-boy or whoever he is really ticked me off. Listen up, Lester."

I couldn't believe what I was hearing. Was this...a little girl talking to me? She sounded twelve years old, max.

"We have a little problem," she said. "And if you don't listen to me closely, it will turn into a big dilemma for you. Craaaaazy big."

"Who are you?" I asked. I still couldn't believe a little girl was threatening me.

"You just received a phone call from a detective at the Saint Louis Police Department, Paranormal Crimes Division," she said, almost whispering. "A Mr. Damian Harris. He's a real pain in the ass, isn't he?"

"How did you know that?"

"You've been out of the game a long time, Lester," she said. "Everybody who's somebody in the supernatural realm knows Damian Harris. It's really unfortunate for me because he's got a nose like a bloodhound, and he's sniffing around in my business. All up in my Kool-Aid, you know? He can't wait to start sniffing you."

"You didn't answer my question," I said. "How did you know that I spoke with the detective?"

"I know everything," she said. "Here's the problem. You *cannot* talk to him. Got it?"

"I can talk to whoever I want," I said. "You're lucky I'm still talking to you."

She clucked her tongue. "Do you know why he wants to talk to you? Probably not...I guess I shouldn't tell you that you're a person of interest."

I paused.

"For what?"

"Oh, I don't know, maybe the fact that you've been fooling around with corpses and demons," she said.

"I don't know what you're talking about," I said.

"Bullshit!" she said, erupting in a roar. "Casino. Visgaroth! Liches! Frank Funeral Home! Undead servant! Jinn! Showdown at the Arch! You need any more proof that I've been watching you?"

She had just rattled off a summary of my last adventure, which was supposed to be a secret.

My phone beeped. Someone was calling my second line. The words PAY PHONE flashed on the caller ID.

Crap.

Hazel barked from the porch.

"That Ant Man on line two?" Bo asked.

I waved him away.

"Terrible timing," he muttered.

"Meet me at the casino," the girl said. "I'll explain. I can help you. But if you meddle in my affairs tonight, you're avocado toast, Lester."

She hung up.

CHAPTER TWO

I LEANED AGAINST THE WALL, bracing myself as if I had been slapped.

Today just got weird. Real weird. Talking to the girl on the phone was like standing in front of a train, and you knew the train was coming, but you didn't want to move because you wanted to know what it would be like to get hit by a train. Jesus.

The last time I met a girl at a casino, it didn't go so well: I ended up running for my life, fighting a blood-thirsty demon, and outsmarting a mysterious gang of jinn—not my idea of fun on a Friday night. Oh, what untold wonders were waiting for me now...

My phone receiver beeped again, pulling me from my confusion. Someone was still on the other line. I clicked over to street static.

"Yo, Les, you gonna come get me?" a voice asked. It was my neighbor, Ant'ny.

Bo grabbed the receiver.

"Where you at?" he asked. He nudged me and motioned to a cradle of pens on the wall. I gave it to him and he wrote something down on the notepad next to the phone feverishly. "We're on the way."

"Well?" Bo asked, replacing the receiver. "Sounds like some shizzle is afoot."

I chugged the last of my cinnamon tea and put my mug in the sink. I grabbed my keys off the hook next to the phone and headed for the porch.

"I don't make choices with a gun held to my head," I said.

"What are you gonna do?" Bo asked.

"Haven't gotten that far yet," I said. "Let's go get Ant'ny."

"If it was me, I'd talk to the cops," Bo said.

I stopped and stared at Bo for several seconds, putting my hands on my hips.

"You were just lecturing me on the virtues of non-cooperation," I said. "Now, all of a sudden, you want me to talk to the police?"

"I'll take jail time any day over whatever that girl's peddling."

"What did she say to you?" I asked.

Bo swatted at me.

"Chick called me a man shrimp, Lester," Bo said.

He made a mocking face as he imitated her voice. "If you think you're going to shield your boss from me, then you're just a little man shrimp. Get Lester on the phone because you're irrelevant, Bo Holloway."

He puffed, standing tall, inflating his chest.

"I was about to say, first, I ain't no man shrimp. Second, *you're* the one that sounds shrimpy. Third—"

My phone rang again.

"No no," I said, opening the porch door. "No more phone calls."

The good Lord himself could have been on that telephone, but I didn't care. I'd had enough ominous phone calls for one day.

My back porch was an add-on sun porch with a thick back

door that led into my kitchen. The kitchen door was the original exterior door. It got very cold and very hot out here, but at least it had windows. My pops and I built it with our own hands fifteen years ago. Actually, I built it, and Pops sat in a chair giving orders. This damn porch almost severely damaged our relationship, but it turned out okay and so did we.

Today was a cool afternoon.

I unhooked my beige gabardine from the wall and slid it on like a man ready for war. Why did I always get dragged into supernatural crap?

I knelt and nuzzled Hazel.

"What was all that barking about, sweet pea?" I asked.

She whined, then offered me a paw, showing the whites of her eyes. I had probably spoken too harshly to her before and I knew better. Hazel was a sensitive one.

I'm a German Shepherd nut. They're the only dog I've ever owned. Years ago, my pops had a heart attack. Pops was on the third floor, and I was in the basement. Our family dog at the time, Rocky, ran all the way downstairs to tell me, and he dragged me by the shirt until I followed him upstairs. Had it not been for his bravery, I would have lost my dad in the prime of his life. I never forgot that. Sure, Hazel chews up my shoes, pees on the floor whenever she meets a friendly stranger, and she sheds enough fur to make a hay farmer blush, but I don't ever doubt her.

I adopted Hazel from the rescue shelter when she was a puppy a few years ago. She's part Labrador and German Shepherd. She's got that Labrador moodiness, but her actions are all German Shepherd, which is what I value in a dog.

"Did you see another squirrel, sweet pea?" I asked.

I spent a minute with her, comforting her and caressing the fur underneath her chin.

Then, her tail shot up. She barked again and crashed into me on her way to the porch windows.

"Hazel!" I said.

She put her front legs on the window sill and woofed, followed by a long growl.

"I don't see anything," Bo said, pulling down a blind.

Pain like lightning surged in my skull, jolting my eyes shut. I staggered backward as a monochrome image whirled across my mind's eye.

I had a gang of undead spiders positioned all over my house to help me spot intruders. I affectionately called them The Cluster. They warned me any time their fight or flight instinct kicked in, beaming me images of what they saw. It's an advanced necromancer's trick.

My porch spider nested under the eave on the back door freaked out.

The image sharpened, and a black shadow hurtled from the sky. My spider skittered as far into the eave as it could.

Still, the shadow loomed closer, eclipsing the rest of the yard. Two angled lines sprouted from the sides of the shadow, moving up and down—furiously.

The shadow zagged to one side, revealing a roll of rippling fur and a horn. A mouth full of sharp teeth opened.

The bat flexed its head forward as it swooped in for the kill.

CHAPTER THREE

Thunk.

I opened my eyes as something slammed against the door.

I whipped the door open and ran outside.

The bat fell toward the grass but rebounded and sped toward the door again.

My spider crouched in the door jamb.

The bat squealed and flew at me. I jumped down the stairs, but it circled and swooped after me.

Hazel bounded out the door and leaped into the air, teeth bared.

The bat dodged Hazel's jaws just in time and flew toward my neighbor's yard before turning around.

Was it rabid? Didn't look like it.

"Stay low!" Bo said.

The bat took a pass at me, and I raised my arm to protect myself.

A searing pain spread down my wrist.

Bo swatted the bat away and it let go of my wrist. A trickle of blood dropped on the steps.

I didn't exactly like the idea of attacking a protected species of animal, but now I didn't have a choice.

The bat shrieked as it circled in for another bite. Hazel growled.

I dashed down the steps underneath my porch that led to my basement door, and I grabbed a dusty tennis racket.

I wrapped both hands around it, ready for a fair fight.

A speckled texture on the underside of my porch drew my gaze upward, and then I screamed.

Hundreds of brown bats hung from the ceiling, staring at me. They crawled over each other, rolling like brown boiling water.

I dove up the stairs as the bats dropped and poured over me.

Bo screamed when he saw them too.

"Motherf—"

"Get down!" I yelled.

Ear-splitting shrieks. The flutter of a thousand wings. My face pressed hard against the cement. The tennis racket pushing against my ribs. My wrist throbbing with pain. Just another night in the life of a necromancer…

A whirlwind of fresh air blasted me, and I looked up.

Bo lay on the ground with his hands over his head. Hazel sat on all fours.

The bats formed a long wand over my garage before arching back toward us.

I put my head down again as they blew past me and through the gangway, into the street, leaving behind a cold, ragged silence.

All three of us lay stunned. All of my spiders were on high alert now, and I felt their fear pulsing in my chest. I willed them to remain in hiding.

"What the hell was that?" I asked, out of breath.

Bo crawled to his knees. His hands immediately went to the back of his neck and rubbed a bite mark.

Hazel whined and licked her back. I rushed to her. I

parted her fur and ran my fingers along a tidy bite mark. I rubbed a drop of her blood between my fingers.

"Bats in daylight," Bo said. "When have you ever seen that?"

"I haven't," I said.

"Huh," Bo said after a moment.

"They bit all of us," I said. "Talk about bad luck."

Bo rubbed his wound. "No blood from me, though. Some bat is probably digesting formaldehyde right now."

Bats were common in my neighborhood. Since many of the homes around here were vacant, the third floors made for nice, warm shelters. You might see a bat or two in the daylight every once in a while, but not hundreds of them out of nowhere.

The universe was trying to tell me something. I've learned that nothing is a coincidence, not when you're a necromancer.

My wrist throbbed. I cupped it with my other hand and glanced at my watch.

"Ant'ny's waiting," I said. "Let's go for a ride, Hazel."

Hazel charged down the walkway that led past my dilapidated weed garden to my detached garage, wagging her tail excitedly. She looked back at me, waiting for me to hurry up.

"You bringing her with us?" Bo asked.

"I'm not leaving her here alone," I said, unwrapping an old leather leash from the iron railing next to the back door.

Before I opened the door to my garage, I regarded my narrow, rectangular backyard, the newest battle scene in my necromancy adventure.

Bo said it best. Shizzle was definitely afoot.

CHAPTER FOUR

I KEPT a first aid kit in my car's glove box. I applied some antiseptic to my wrist and covered the bite marks with a bandage, wincing as my flesh wound stung.

I put a bandage on the back of Bo's neck. With his bald, fatty head, he looked like Ving Rhames's character from *Pulp Fiction*. He didn't like that reference too much.

But, boy, was it nice to be away from my house, cruising down my alley, and then into the streets of my city.

Despite everything we'd just been through, my '93 Lincoln Town Car's cruise factor was like comfort food. Tan paint, chestnut-colored soft top, windows down, and the breeze blowing oh so fine, baby.

Bo drove my car like he owned it—slumped back, one hand on the steering wheel.

Hazel poked her head out the rear driver's side window, her tongue flailing.

I had Lonnie Liston Smith & the Cosmic Echoes' classic 1976 jazz album, *Renaissance*, in the tape deck. Good introspective jazz album, one my pops and I used to listen to on starry nights. Lonnie put a crazy effect on his keyboard that made it sound like he was playing jazz piano at the bottom of the ocean. Kind of matched how I felt. It was the kind of thinking music I needed. My jazz drove Bo nuts, and under normal circumstances, he would have taken the opportunity to school me on the virtues of rap. This time, he left me alone to think.

My neighborhood was all masonry, trees, and grass. Boulevards full of three-story brick houses and empty lots where weeds and tall grass swayed over the foundations of what used to be the city's most historic homes.

If you want to know what an inner-city neighborhood looks like, all you have to do is drive down any of the streets around here: renovated houses next to condemned houses next to burned out houses with boards over every window next to block-long empty lots, with liquor stores and storefront churches on the ends. And don't forget the discount cigarette shops, chop suey restaurants, and loan sharks—that's Academy/Sherman Park for you.

We turned onto Martin Luther King Boulevard. Rush hour. Stop-and-go traffic and strings of ruby brake lights for blocks. The Metro bus dropped folks off from work, slowing everything down. If you had somewhere to be, there was nothing worse than getting stuck behind the 4:15 bus. It rumbled and stopped, rumbled and stopped, its hydraulics whooshing as it rose up and down.

A bird flew overhead, making me think of the bats. Who sent them? What did the bite marks mean?

I still hadn't even had time to reflect on the decision I had to make: talk to the police or meet the girl at the casino?

The older I get, the more I realize there aren't easy answers. It seems like everything gets more ambiguous every year you're alive, like God's way of keeping things interesting so you don't become wise without working at it. My neighbor, Granny, put it poetically: around my age, you gotta start showing the youngsters the reason you've been alive so long, so help you Gawd.

I wasn't choosing between right and wrong. This was like

heartburn, and I was choosing between ibuprofen and antacids to treat it. Both got the job done, but you couldn't take them at the same time.

The most relevant question was, who did I prefer to piss off?

Yeah, not the police. I could handle whoever was on the phone. I didn't want to handle jail time, though. Funny how a little thinking time gives you some clarity that you should have had all along.

"I'm going to talk to the detective," I said.

Bo nodded triumphantly as we slowed down for a red light. "Good call, boss man."

"For the record, you were against this before you were for it," I said.

"A sensible brother is entitled to change his mind," Bo said.

The light switched to green and he cut a quick left and into a parking lot under construction next to a masonry building with an empty storefront.

A crew of construction workers gathered around the tailgate of a black pickup truck, drinking water from plastic cups.

Bo honked and popped the trunk. One of the workers in a red hoodie, jeans, and work boots saw us and waved. He lugged a toolbox out of the back of the truck. He threw his tools in my trunk and launched himself into my backseat.

"How was school, baby?" Bo said jokingly. "What'd you learn today?"

"Sup, fellas."

Anthony Rice lived directly across the street from me. His family let him move back in a couple of years ago after getting out of prison. Marijuana possession with an intent to sell. He got six years, but they let him out on parole after three. His parole ended last year, thank goodness. At thirty-seven, Ant'ny made some bad mistakes, but he still had a good heart.

"Crazy traffic today," he said, rubbing his goatee. Hazel nudged him. "What's up, Hazel?"

"Sorry we're late," Bo said. "We got attacked by a flock of bats."

Ant'ny's eyes went wide.

"Just kiddin'," Bo said, easing the car in a smooth, backward circle. "It was the 4:15 bus."

Ant'ny didn't know about my necromancy. No one in my neighborhood did.

So you're probably thinking, how did I explain Bo? You know, why a six-foot-tall man-mountain was living in my house all of a sudden?

I said he was my wife's cousin who came to live with me. I downplayed the fact that he smelled a little funny. Nobody could quite place the faint but lingering smell of embalming fluid and rotting flesh. It's a unique assault on the nostrils, and you ought to be glad that this adventure isn't available in a scratch-and-sniff edition.

"How was work?" I asked, changing the subject as Bo eased out of the parking lot.

"Just about finished," Ant'ny said. "Once we're done, the Second Chance Center will be able to move in. The city wouldn't let any moving trucks in until we redid the parking lot."

Ant'ny worked for a contractor who did construction work for all the inner-city nonprofits in town. He was a day laborer, about the only job he could get in this part of town being an ex-con.

He bent forward and poked the bandage on the back of Bo's head. "You get into a fight?"

"Don't ask," Bo said.

A wide grin spread across Ant'ny's face. "You look like Ving Rhames from that one movie."

"Ha ha," Bo said, frowning.

"Just because you don't like it doesn't make it any less true," I said.

"You're saying I'm Lucifer," Bo said.

"Whoa, didn't nobody say that, man," Ant'ny said.

"I read that on the internet once," Bo said. "Fan theories."

"I take it back then, damn," Ant'ny said. "You can't take a joke tonight."

He pulled on my seat.

"You got a bandage too, Lester," Ant'ny said, tapping my seat. "What the hell were you both doing together?"

"Pure coincidence," Bo said.

When silence fell between us, Ant'ny settled back in his seat and said, "Y'all are weird sometimes. You still up for cards?"

"Can't," I said. "I'm meeting someone back at the house."

"Dang, man," he said. "You in, Bo?"

"Depends," Bo said.

"You both are acting weird today," Ant'ny said. "Let me guess: you robbed a bank."

"Robbed it dry," I said. "We can't share any of the money with you either."

"We spent it all on a hacienda in Mexico," Bo said.

"Y'all are something else," Ant'ny said.

I laughed. "That's one way of putting it."

Silence grew between us as Bo drove.

"Seriously, though," Ant'ny said, "you're not going to tell me anything?"

Bo slowed down for a red light.

A baby blue hatchback pulled up next to us.

You know how sometimes you drive on autopilot and you see things without actually seeing them?

For example, you see people's license plates, but you don't read them. You see people at a crosswalk, but you don't pay attention to their faces. You pass by the same buildings every day, but you don't actually know what they look like.

But even then, you *know* when something is missing. If the church you pass every day gets painted, you notice. If a telephone pole is cracked in half, you notice. Our eyes are masters at spotting breaks in everyday patterns.

So imagine the look on my face when I noticed that the blue hatchback didn't have *a driver.*

I craned my head to get a better look. There wasn't a single soul in any of the pristine leather seats.

Another hatchback pulled up next to Bo. It was also empty.

I nudged Bo.

"Call me crazy, but neither car to the side of us has any passengers," I whispered.

Bo glanced over.

"I'll be damned," he said.

In the rearview mirror, another hatchback pulled to a stop. No one inside.

Sure enough, the car in front of us was an empty hatchback too.

Same make and model, same baby blue color.

"Shizzle," I said.

"Mmm-hmm," Bo said, wrinkling his lips. "Shizzle."

"Shizzle what?" Ant'ny asked. Then he noticed the hatchbacks.

"Look at those babies," he said. "Are those Teslas? They don't look like it. Wait, where the drivers at?"

The light turned green.

The front car pulled forward. Bo followed, and the other cars rolled with us down the street.

The turn-off into my subdivision was one block away.

Bo gunned the accelerator and tried to cut off the hatchback on the left. The hatchback accelerated, blocking Bo's attempt. The front car braked hard, forcing him to a stop.

The cars hemmed us in.

"Watch it, Bo!" Ant'ny yelled.

Traffic honked at us.

Bo accelerated cautiously, and we missed our turn. My subdivision slid by and into the rearview mirror. We had no choice but to continue down the road.

We had been followed—and taken hostage—by *driverless cars*. As they guided us onto the highway, there was only one destination we could be going to—the casino.

CHAPTER FIVE

I wondered how many people noticed our entourage as we sped onto the interstate in rush hour traffic. Then again, it wouldn't have mattered because we weren't causing any trouble. The hatchbacks made sure of that, tracking us on both sides so that we couldn't change lanes.

The first glimmers of twilight streaked the sky as we rolled off the highway toward a square glass tower with a shimmering neon shell—it looked like a skewed photograph frame. The casino hotel. Night was falling fast.

"I want answers," Ant'ny said. We had avoided his questions so far, but he wasn't accepting our silence anymore. "This kinda thing doesn't happen every day!"

I sighed. Maybe picking him up from work was a bad idea. I couldn't have known in retrospect that we'd have a supernatural encounter.

"Look, Ant'ny," I said, "Bo and I got mixed up with some bad people. It looks like they want a meeting. Just stay quiet and you'll be fine."

"Bad people?" Ant'ny asked. "Who, the Mafia?"

"Yeah, the driverless, electric car Mafia," Bo joked.

"I have no idea, actually," I said. "That's what makes this whole thing strange."

"What did y'all do?" Ant'ny asked. His eyes went wide at an internal revelation. "Y'all *did* rob a bank!"

"Not quite," I said. "More like we were in the wrong place at the wrong time."

Hazel lay in the backseat, bored. Ant'ny patted her.

"It's all right, Hazel," he said. "I'll take care of you when the police haul these fools to jail."

"I wouldn't mind police right now," I said.

Bo turned into the casino property, and the cars led him around the parking lot. The place was busy tonight. Valets jogged back and forth under the porte-cochere as folks handed them the keys and strode through the elegant glass doors to the casino lobby. Inside, glowing neon chandeliers pulsed in pastel colors.

Just before the entrance, the cars steered us into another lane that led around the casino and toward a covered parking garage.

I groaned.

That garage brought back painful memories. The last time I was there, I got jumped and thrown in a trunk.

We entered the garage and climbed to the top floor where a skywalk led to the hotel.

The front car's hazard lights flashed as it braked.

The other cars braked next to us, stopping so close that we could barely open the doors.

We waited in silence until a computerized voice blared from a speaker in the ceiling.

"Step out of the car."

"Should we run for it?" Bo asked.

"If you run, you die," the computer voice said. "Step out of the car."

Bo, Ant'ny, and I opened our doors. I had to hop out because my door was only a few inches from the nearest hatchback. I banged my knee on the edge of the car door and grimaced. Ghosts of my old knee injury flared up.

"Rear passenger, return to the car," the computer said.

Ant'ny put on a "why me?" face.

"Return to the car if you know what's good for you," the voice said.

"Get back in, Ant'ny," I said. "We'll be back."

"Maybe," Bo muttered.

"Look after Hazel," I said.

Hazel tilted her head at me as I waved to her and told her to stay and protect the car.

"Proceed to the sliding door entrance directly ahead," the voice said. "The cars surrounding you are rigged with dynamite, and they will explode if you think about doing anything stupid."

Even if the voice was bluffing, it wasn't worth taking a chance. Bo and I entered a sliding automatic door into the skywalk connecting the casino and the garage.

An elevator dinged and the doors opened into a car with mirrors on the walls and ceiling. I knew this elevator, but I had never ridden it past the skywalk level.

The elevator carried us to the top floor of the hotel. We were so high up, the elevator wobbled as it came to a stop.

The elevator dinged open, and we walked into a velvet-wallpapered hallway. The walls were the color of flesh. Subtle red line lights in the walls glowed like veins, forking up and down the wall.

Several double doors lined the hallway. Looked like suites.

"Enter the door at the end of the hallway," the voice said. I spotted several security cameras on the ceiling staring at us.

We reached brown double doors at the end of the hallway. Two more cameras were angled in the corner above the door.

Inside, a lavish penthouse suite overlooked the Arch and the Mississippi River. Through the long, floor-to-ceiling windows, the riverfront buildings were lighting up one by one, as a navy sky darkened the fading sunlight.

The terraced living room had an expensive gray couch with colorful accent pillows.

"Sit down," the voice said.

Bo and I took a seat on the couch in front of a huge flat screen TV.

The TV flickered on, displaying a photograph of Bo and me sitting in my car, puzzled looks on our faces. It was from a few minutes ago when we were taken hostage.

Yellow handwritten text appeared on the screen, slapped across the bottom: GREATEST PRANK OF ALL TIME?

A play button appeared in the middle of the screen.

Click.

A table. Camera looking down it.

A cardboard box appeared with a glissando sound effect.

Two hands with red, glittery nails curved onto the screen from off-camera, wiggling their fingers over the box.

"Oooh, I've been waiting for this!"

It was the girl who called me earlier—she narrated the video.

The screen cut to the box opened, with packing peanuts all over the table.

The hands pulled out a gold foil-wrapped rectangle as an angel choir sound effect chimed.

Cut to the square being unwrapped like a candy bar.

Cut to the hands tossing the paper off-camera.

VHS tape.

The hands held it up to the camera to show the title written in a red permanent marker, all caps.

THE STORY OF THE GOOD NECROMANCER.

The camera followed the hands as they floated through a green pastel bedroom to a VCR.

The VCR hummed and whirred.

Scraggly static on an old TV. Rewind. Screeching snow. Shadows whirling backward....

"This is going to be good!"

The camera zoomed into the old TV screen.

An invisible hand holding a pencil drew on graph paper in black ink.

A stick figure with curly hair.

"This story starts with a necromancer named Lester Broussard," the girl said, and a sound effect of kids cheering played. "Let's do a study in human nature, mmm? Here's Lester's lovely wife. Isn't she beautiful?"

I stared as the hand drew a stick figure image of my wife. I was ready to punch a hole through the television. But I couldn't stop watching as an invisible eraser rubbed my wife's lower half. A caption bubble with the words HELP appeared over her head.

"Cancer sucks," the girl said. "Especially when you have two kids."

The hand drew hardscrabble stick figures of my children, Marcus and Marlese, with sad faces.

The girl put on a movie announcer voice. "In a world of unfair harshness, a family teeters on the verge of despair."

She clucked her tongue and laughed.

"Lester's wife was fading away. Lester was overwhelmed with grief. So sad. Some people learn to accept death. Some people never accept it. And others embrace it...ooooh, here's another pretty woman."

A crude image of my friend CeCe stood next to my figure.

"A chance encounter. A deviant woman with a fetish for the dead shows our hero the promise of necromancy. Forbidden secrets! Corpse manipulation! Black magic! In it, maybe he can find a cure to his wife's cancer."

She scribbled a pentagram. It glowed in blue and green. My image moved into the middle of it with captions popping over my head.

I WON'T ACCEPT DEATH.
I WON'T LET MY WIFE BE JUST A MEMORY.
I'LL DO WHATEVER IT TAKES.

The hand drew a giant scorpion demon next to me, and it moved from side to side as the girl impersonated Visgaroth's deep voice.

"Swear allegiance to me and I will give you a cure for your wife's cancer, Lester Broussard. Rawhrrr!"

Caption over my head: I ACCEPT.

"And now, our friend Lester became one of the powerful necromancers in history under Visgaroth's tutelage..."

My wife's lower half appeared again.

Caption. HONEY, IT'S A MIRACLE!

The demon laughed and a black cloud appeared over my head, raining animated blood.

Thunder. Lightning. The canvas shook as the scorpion's tail struck my wife.

The girl impersonated a scream.

LESTER!!!

My image dropped to his knees.

NOOO...

Demon laughter.

"Betrayal!" the girl said, erasing my wife and drawing a gravestone in her place.

My son's image hovered over the gravestone.

"The sins of the father! Suddenly, necromancy becomes a family profession..."

The scorpion hovered over Marcus as a black cloud appeared over his head.

The scorpion slashed him and the hand erased him.

Caption over my head as I faceplant into the graph paper: WHAT HAVE I DONE???

"What else could a mere mortal have expected other than the fuck-up of the century? Everyone knows demons lie..."

My daughter's image slid next to me.

"Our sweet Marlese escaped death, but her first experience with necromancy was watching her brother die while summoning Visgaroth. What's it like for an innocent teenage girl to realize that her father destroyed the family with black magic? Oh my..."

Marlese inched away from me and the hand drew a red X between us as my daughter faded away.

My heart might as well have been a steel weight.

"Seven years of solitude," the girl said, scribbling the number seven and doodling flowers around it. "Seven solemn years before our poor necromancer would return to the dark arts and show us why he's the greatest necromancer of all time."

A giant can of bug spray appeared and sprayed the scorpion. It curled up as the girl erased it.

"What's not to admire about our dear Lester Broussard?"

The graph paper background burned away to grainy video footage of my house. I was in my bathrobe picking up the morning paper.

Then the video cut to security camera footage of me playing blackjack at the casino, leaned over the table and a shell of myself. Then it cut to another camera on the other side of the casino floor, with me and a woman in black running from something.

Then the film cut to the St. Louis Riverfront. I climbed out of the Mississippi River, drenched and breathing heavily. The camera froze on my exhausted face and zoomed in.

A bell dinged. "Who's the man behind all that grief?" the girl asked. "Why has he chosen to use the dark arts for good? What kind of unselfish monster does that—like, really? Only the greatest of all time!"

The tape stopped and the TV flashed off.

Bo's jaw dropped.

I was shaking in fear and in rage.

"Wasn't that amazing?" a voice said.

The girl. She was in the room.

Bo and I jumped up, looking around. We didn't see anyone.

"Come out!" I yelled.

"Forgive me, but I'm fangirling," the girl said. "I want to savor this moment."

A swivel chair near the window revolved to face us.

A short woman in a red leather beret and a loose-fitting pink turtleneck sweater stared at us. She wasn't a little girl, but she could have passed for one.

She tipped down huge, bulbous sunglasses to see us better with red-veined eyes.

"Can I at least get a round of applause for that entrance?" she asked, smiling—revealing two dagger-sharp fangs.

CHAPTER SIX

I haven't had too many run-ins with vampires. They tend to stay away from necromancers, and vice versa. The disdain is mutual.

Necromancers manipulate the dead. Vampires live forever and never experience death.

When I die, I'll go to the spirit world. When a vampire is killed, they'll turn to dust.

I heard of a legendary feud between a necromancer and a vampire that happened a long time ago—in Europe, I think. They hated each other's guts. The vampire bit the necromancer's love and turned her immortal, forever robbing the necromancer of spending the afterlife with her. As revenge, the necromancer traveled to the spirit world, made a shadow deal with a demon and bound every lover the vampire ever had, and created an army of undead servants. He made the vampire watch as they served him—and, if the myth is true, there might have been a sexual act or two.

The lovers descended on the vampire and drove stakes through his heart. The act of controlling so many undead shattered the necromancer's mind and killed him too.

Necromancers and vampires have avoided each other ever since.

Whether the legend is true or not, I prefer not to associate myself with the bloodsuckers. Nothing good can ever come from hanging around vampires, and I dare you to prove me wrong.

Bo pointed at the vampire and scowled. "You the one that called me a man shrimp?"

"You bet your shrimpy ass I did," the woman said, rising.

"Vampire," Bo said, charging her, "meet window."

Bo reared back a fist and threw a hard punch.

The vampire caught Bo's fist with her palm and cupped her hand around it, stopping him cold. He yelled as she twisted his fist and brought him to his knees.

"I stand by what I said," she said, grinning.

Bo rose and tried to rush her with his free hand, but she grabbed him, swung him around, and launched him like a discus. He smashed into the wall and landed on a wicker chair, flattening it.

"Man shrimp, meet wall," she said, throwing her hands up victoriously. She pretended to switch between sports announcer voices. "Well, Bob, that's what you call a gold medal throw. Yes, indeed, Jimmy, I'd say that guy is having sweet dreams right now..."

She laughed, hopping her way up the terraced floor toward me.

"Now that we can chat uninterrupted," she said, extending a hand, "how are you, Lester?"

I stared at her hand, then at her face. She couldn't have been taller than five feet. Even though I despised her on sight, there was something intoxicating about her eyes—they had that vampire gleam. I'd heard stories of people falling in love with vampires, only to get their hearts broken, and their blood sucked. I broke eye contact.

"Fine," she said, shrugging. "Help yourself to a drink if

you want one. I promise there's no poison. I won't keep you long."

She gestured to a wet bar replete with tall, colorful bottles of wine. I didn't move. Bo groaned from the other side of the room.

This woman was nuts. I was sure of it.

"You better start talking," I said.

"Or what?" she asked, grinning her fangs again. "I could put you through the window and laugh as you plummet to your death."

"Why haven't you done it yet?" I asked.

The vampire sauntered over to the bar and poured herself a glass of red wine. At least, it looked like wine.

"Because I hoped that we could come to a mutual understanding," she said. She swirled the glass. "You see, I respect the hell out of you, Lester. Call me a pupil of your skills. I've studied your techniques and I know you're the real deal. But guess what? So am I! I did my best to show you that I'm not a threat you want to mess with. You. Do. Not. Want. To. Screw. With. Me. Seriously. I also want you to know that I recognize and respect your power, Lester. Hopefully, that means something to you."

She sipped her drink, circling the glass with her wrist. "The name's Fiona by the way."

I didn't let her compliments get to me. However flattering they were, she meant harm.

"Why go through all this to get to me?" I asked.

"Because I had to do my research," she said. "You don't exactly like to pick up the phone."

"How did you know all of those things about me?" I asked. I was still shaken by the video.

"A few deals with demons and good old surveillance," she said. "You've been out of the game for a long time. You aren't hard to follow."

Something told me I needed to do a better job paying attention to my surroundings.

"I called you here to extend a peace offering," Fiona said.

"Don't start none, won't be none, like they say in the hood," I said. "And the last time somebody extended me a 'peace offering,' it didn't end well. Maybe you ought to have done better research."

Fiona nearly choked on her wine, laughing condescendingly at me. "Oooh, the threats are in full swing now!"

She walked along the window, sipping her wine. How old was she? With vampires, you never knew. She had a carefree walk. Reminded me of a kitten playing with a ball of yarn before skewering it.

"In a few hours, I'm going to rearrange the very fabric of the supernatural world," she said. "It's going to be epic, and it doesn't concern you. I know your tendencies, Lester. You're the kind that will involve yourself in my affairs and make things difficult for me. You and the police both. I don't want to start a feud, so I'm asking you to stay home. Lock your doors, disconnect your phone, do absolutely nothing until tomorrow morning. If you do that for me, then you'll wake up tomorrow and you'll continue your nice life with your man shrimp, dog, and a cluster of dead spiders. Most importantly, you will *live*."

"I...ain't no...shrimp," Bo said, trying to stagger up. He fell face-first into the carpet and cursed at his weakness.

"Sounds to me like a villain monologue," I said. "If you knew me so well, you wouldn't threaten me."

A frown spread across her face.

"Lester, do you have any idea what it's like to endure this...this...bullshit?"

"Define bullshit."

"Vampirism," she said, refreshing her glass. "I didn't ask for this."

"You got turned against your will," I said. "I get it. What about it?"

"I was a sophomore in college. A fucking sophomore!"

She faced the Arch.

"My future was taken away from me. I mean, maybe there wasn't much of a future, with student loans and crappy internships. I had zero clue what I was going to do with my life other than getting a marketing degree. And then—boom. Two fangs in my neck and I'm relegated to darkness and blood. There isn't a degree that will prepare you for this lifestyle, you know."

She put a palm on the glass, a look of desperation and hurt on her face.

"For a long time, I cried from dusk to dawn, asking God, why me? I refused to feed for a while, but I had to learn to kill. I dreamed of walking in the sunlight...Just strolling across the college lawns, getting in a car, and driving nowhere at all, with the sunshine on my face and the radio blaring. I miss my old life."

A sudden rage washed over her and she hardened. She threw her wine glass on the carpet, staining it forever red. She stomped on the glass with red leather boots and ground the shards into the soiled carpet. She pivoted at me, fangs bared.

"I refuse to let this define me!" she cried. "I am *not* just some pretty vampire. Everything changes tonight."

She stalked toward me, determination on her face. She was scaring me now.

"You're a good necromancer," she said. "Kind of an oxymoron, but you understand. You use your powers for good. I'm going to follow in your footsteps. I'm going to be a good vampire, Lester."

She brushed past me on her way to the door.

"Tonight is the last night I drink blood, forever. It is the last night I hide in the shadows. Tonight, I take back my life, and my future."

"Good for you," I said. "Or not."

Fiona threw open the double doors to the penthouse. "I've

found a cure to vampirism, Lester. And tonight, I am going to unleash it on the world."

CHAPTER SEVEN

Fiona motioned to someone in the hallway.

"Loves, it's time to escort our friends home!"

A dozen or so vampires had lined up in the hallway, waiting for us.

They were all young—none of them past thirty from what I can tell. Dressed for a fashion shoot. Make-up—even on the males. Bold colors, scarves, and leather—lots of leather. They were magazine cover-ready, that's for sure.

"Get your man shrimp and come with me," Fiona barked.

I helped Bo up. His tracksuit rubbed against my arm as he staggered up.

"Speak of this to no one," Bo whispered. "Ant'ny will never let me live this down."

"We're good," I said, patting him on the back.

"Don't you like what we've done with the place?" Fiona asked, motioning us to follow.

"If you mean making the walls look like veins, then no," I said, giving the walls another glance as we passed into the hallway. This hotel was supposed to be a Four Seasons. Didn't look like it anymore. The energy was different. Almost Satanic.

"I guess you could say we did a hostile takeover," Fiona said. "Is it weird that the hottest casino and hotel in town are owned by a millennial vampire?"

"Millennial?" I asked. "How old *are* you?"

"I was twenty when I was bitten," Fiona said. "I've been infected for…two years, I think."

"Infected sounds about right to me," Bo said under his breath.

"You're twenty years old?" I asked, incredulous. "I want proof."

Fiona shrugged. "Do I look older than that to you?"

"My God," I said.

I was being threatened and held hostage by a twenty-year-old. When I was her age, I was working a full-time job trying to afford a wedding ring. World domination wasn't even in my vocabulary. Kids these days. Sheeeeeet…

The elevator at the end of the hallway dinged open.

We crowded in with Fiona and several of her vamps and rode the car down to the casino floor. A wall of cigarette smoke hit us as the doors opened. We followed her to the casino floor.

"We can't change very much on the casino floor, of course," Fiona said, gesturing to the bright neon lights and swarms of people around roulette tables. Eighties music played on speakers overhead.

The last time I was here, I was drinking a Scotch and soda at the blackjack table, and I had no idea that I'd be back to my old supernatural ways.

"Isn't this place amazing, Lester?" Fiona asked. "On a packed night, it's like you're in the center of the world."

"You don't strike me as the gambling type," I said.

"You're right," she said. "But look carefully at all these people. Are they actually gambling?"

A man in a baseball cap laid down his cards at the blackjack table. At a roulette table, a croupier spun a roulette wheel and a crowd of people cheered. An old woman smoking a slim cigarette pulled a lever at a slot machine, and an orchestra hit sounded as the reel whirled with images of cherries, sevens, and gold coins.

I put on a long face. "If these people aren't gambling, then what do you call it?"

Fiona sighed. "You can't see it."

"You're nuts," Bo said. "I see that very clearly."

"They're *praying*," Fiona said with another arrogant sigh.

The comparison took me off-guard. People did a lot of things when they gambled. Praying was definitely one of them. But I wouldn't have called the entire act itself prayer.

"Every blow on the dice is an offering to this place," Fiona said. "Everyone comes here with money in their pockets. The money stays, they go. Yet this casino is so…empty. Spiritually, I mean. What if I could change that?"

"You're not the first person to try to 'save' casinos," I said. "It can't be done."

"I don't care about morality," Fiona said. "If people want to gamble themselves stupid, that's their choice. But I win when they do."

She laughed.

"I will rearrange my relationship with blood," she said. "I will swap it with gambling. When people come to this casino, I will feed on their offerings. I'll no longer need blood. Vice will keep me alive."

"That's ridiculous," I said. "And impossible."

"A few shadow deals say otherwise," Fiona said. "Do you know what kind of bargains I had to make to get to this point? It would make you shudder. But because I'm a vampire, I can command better deals."

"Vampires can't talk to the dead," I said. "You can't visit the spirit world. How did you—"

Fiona laughed. "It doesn't matter now. But I should thank you for getting rid of Visgaroth for me."

She led us down an aisle of slot machines.

"He and I made a deal," Fiona said. "It came with a lot of nasty conditions. I was certain he was going to betray me. Right around the time we took over this place, we noticed some strange activity on the security cameras. Turns out it was *you*. Luckily, I got what I needed from him before you exterminated him. I got all the benefits of a shadow deal without the unpleasant consequences. I was impressed with you, and I did my research."

She circled back to the elevators. I wondered what this tour was all about.

We rode the car up to the parking garage. The doors opened and Fiona held them for us.

We emerged into the parking garage where several vampires leaned against the blue hatchbacks. In the backseat of my car, Ant'ny and Hazel were sitting on high alert. Ant'ny waved when he saw us.

"Remember my offer," Fiona said. "Stay home tonight, Lester. This transformation has nothing to do with you, and it won't affect you when it's complete."

Fiona snapped. The vampires leaned away from the hatchbacks, and the cars pulled forward, unblocking my car.

"Get in my way, and you're dead," she said.

"And you call yourself an aspiring good vampire?" I asked.

"Once my plans are complete, I'll never touch another neck again," Fiona said. "Isn't that a definition of good?"

"I just got one question," Bo said. He pursed his lips and pointed at her. "And I want to know the answer, all right?"

Silence. Fiona folded her arms and stared at him through her giant sunglasses.

"Of all the cars in the world, why'd you have to send hatchbacks after us?" Bo asked.

"They're hybrids," she said. "Besides, I like the look."

Bo raised an eyebrow. "You are one weird chick."

"Bye, Lester," she snapped. "I sure hope we don't meet

again. Now get the hell out of my casino and go home where you belong."

She strode through the sliding glass door, her red leather beret bobbing as she walked, and her vampires followed her.

Throughout all of this, I couldn't stop thinking: Why me? What is her angle?

"Wait," I said.

She stopped without turning around.

"You said you know me," I said. "Do you think I'm going to go home and hide?"

"Not for all the poker chips in the world," she said. "But if you're going to mess with me, consider yourself warned."

The automatic doors shut behind her.

CHAPTER EIGHT

Bo peeled out of the parking garage. He almost collided with a few cars on his way down the ramp, but I didn't yell at him. I wanted him to go faster.

I half expected our car to blow up or get riddled with machine guns before we left the casino property—this journey was getting weirder by the minute and I didn't trust Fiona's mental state enough to expect her *not* to try and kill us.

Bo and I both let out a collective sigh of relief as we burst out of the parking lot and made distance between us and the casino. We merged onto the highway and floored it.

We might as well have been driving with our eyes in the rearview mirror—I swear, if I had seen a single driverless hatchback, I would have freaked out. I scanned the driver's seat of every car that whizzed by.

"I think we're clear," I said, resting my head against my seat and closing my eyes. We were out of the downtown epicenter now and back in the hood. Bo turned off the interstate.

Hazel whimpered in the backseat.

"Nice to know y'all can communicate," Ant'ny said.

He was *mad*. I knew my neighbor. Ant'ny didn't like secrets being hidden from him. I owed him an explanation, but he couldn't handle the truth. I wasn't sure if *I* could handle the truth right now.

"Who was that woman?" he asked.

"No idea," I said. "And I mean that. She threatened me something awful, though."

"Mafia?" Ant'ny asked.

"Before we met her, I would have said no," I said. "But now that I think about it, Mafia isn't a bad way to explain her."

"She called me a man shrimp," Bo said, complaining. He shook his head and mocked her voice under his breath.

I turned to Ant'ny.

"Look. I know that it seems like we're holding back on you. And I would be mad if I were you too. But trust me when I say you want no part of this. I'm just trying to keep you safe. This is life or death stuff, Ant'ny."

Ant'ny took a deep breath, sighed, and then gave me a fist bump.

"A'ight, but as far as I'm concerned, you're still the black Mr. Rogers."

Bo cackled. "I know that's right!"

I petted Hazel, ignoring the comment. Normally, it would have bristled me.

"You probably need to go to the bathroom, don't you, sweet pea?" I asked.

"Her and me both," Ant'ny said. "And I want some food."

I nodded and waved to Bo. "Let's stop for a minute."

Bo turned into a local fried chicken joint, a garish white building with vinyl siding, red shutters, and a slanted roof. The place looked like a literal chicken, tucked between houses with bars over the windows. This was where you came when you wanted *real* fried chicken that wasn't your mama's or your grandmama's. The air around the place might as well have had a grease index, the smell was so potent. But it sure did smell good.

Ant'ny and Bo wandered in for some dinner.

I took Hazel to a grassy patch next to the postage stamp parking lot and waited for her to do her business.

I dug my hands into my gabardine and watched the cars pass by. The stars were bright and the air was warm and humid. A classic St. Louis night. Somewhere, a dog barked—probably sensed Hazel.

We were far enough away from Fiona to be safe now. I hoped.

What did all of this mean?

I still hadn't processed that video yet. Anyone who made a video like that with your whole life story in it to threaten you meant serious business. They were probably ten thousand steps ahead of you too.

Curing vampirism...

What the hell did I care if vampires disappeared from the world tomorrow? They weren't exactly holy. How many people's lives would improve for the better? For starters, you could walk down a dark alley in the middle of the night and at least know that becoming a vampire wouldn't be one of the possible dangers you could face. I'd call that a win.

Fiona herself said she was turned against her will in college. I couldn't imagine what that would be like, to be so young and have your whole life ripped away from you like that. At least necromancy was a choice. Being turned into a vampire was like a supernatural assault. In that respect, I understood Fiona.

But there was something about her that I couldn't place. Something unsettling that made my stomach wrench into knots. Maybe this was a normal reaction from meeting a vampire, but I wasn't sure.

Hazel wandered across the parking lot, her head down low and her nose sniffing like crazy. I followed her, told her to stay away from a dead bird.

I looked back at the restaurant windows. Ant'ny emerged from the bathroom. Bo was waiting in line to order. He patted the back of his neck where the bandage was, and then he rubbed it like it itched.

At that same moment, the bite marks on my wrist burned. Searing pain tore up my arm and I broke into an instant sweat.

I grabbed my wrist and massaged it, but the pain worsened. The fried chicken joint blurred across my vision. I needed to sit down.

The first aid kit in my glove box. I had some medicine in there. I had to get to it...

I stumbled toward the car. The pain spread to my head now, and my temples throbbed.

A thud stopped me.

Hazel collapsed into the grass.

I pivoted back toward her, but my knees gave out and I toppled into the grass, my arm around her back.

I happened to glance at the restaurant. Inside, Bo crashed into a table and Ant'ny dashed toward him.

I settled into the ground, breathing heavily. Hazel's warmth radiated next to me. I became one with the grass, the stars, the cars speeding by, the cloud of invisible grease, and the dog barking in the distance...I closed my eyes.

∽

RAWRK!

RAWRK!

I came to. The stars and the grass and the cars passing by blurred into the focus.

I lay in the grass. Hazel barked at me.

I inhaled.

Hazel grabbed my jacket sleeve and tugged.

"Hey now, Hazel," I said groggily.

I pulled myself to my knees. They didn't like that very much. I pushed myself to my feet, ignoring the needles of pain in my knees.

Every car that sped by sent a vicious wind in my direction. Hazel's bark echoed louder than normal. The world swirled around me like water in a cup.

My car was a couple of feet away, the passenger side door still open—just how I left it.

"C'mon," I said, wobbling as I motioned to Hazel. "Let's sit down and wait for Bo and Ant'ny."

I just needed to sit down for a minute, catch my breath.

We walked through the humid air toward the car. The door opened and echoed across the parking lot.

I pointed inside, but Hazel wouldn't get in.

"C'mon, sweet pea," I said. "I'm not in the mood to chase you around today. Get in the car."

Hazel sat and stared at me, her head cocked.

"Hazel," I said in a fatherly tone.

And then I realized she wasn't staring at me. She was staring past me.

An enormous cave sat where the fried chicken joint should have been. It was like a beach cavern—tall with a skinny opening. Rocky brown peaks jutted into the navy sky.

"So this is a dream," I said, throwing up my hands. "What other untold wonders await us tonight?"

My wrist burned, the pain dull this time.

"You're not scared, Hazel?" I asked.

Hazel put her nose low to the ground, sniffed, and trotted toward the darkness.

If anybody had reason to be scared, it would be Hazel.

Grabbing my wrist, I stalked toward the cavern and let her lead the way.

I used to spend long evenings watching Hazel sniffing around outside, fascinated by how she reacted to things. A dog's sense of smell is their best asset, and to be in a new place is exhilarating for them. They smell things that we couldn't even imagine.

I wondered what she was smelling now as we entered the cavern's maw. The temperature dropped and the noises from the neighborhood were distant echoes now.

If only I had a torch. It was dark as hell in here. Couldn't see a thing.

My ears became hyper-aware, and the only thing I could hear was Hazel's footsteps ahead of me and her nose working full-time.

"Don't run away from me," I said.

I leaned down and grabbed her collar so I could keep track of her. It didn't seem to matter to her because she pulled me along as if I were nothing.

She stopped. Sniffed. Stopped. Sniffed.

I tripped over a rock and cursed as I righted myself.

A dim orange light appeared in the distance, hovering in the darkness. At least we had something to focus on now.

Hazel stopped, and I bumped into her.

"What is it?" I whispered.

She sniffed.

I stepped forward and my shoe stepped in something mushy.

Mud?

No.

Didn't smell like it.

Hazel sniffed.

I sniffed and caught a whiff of something foul. It immediately wrinkled up my nose and I put on a stank face.

God, this stuff smelled horrible. Almost like...ammonia?

Something scratched the rock above us.

I looked up but didn't see anything.

Slowly, I backed up and pulled Hazel with me.

Scratch. Scratch. Scratch.

Something was immediately above us.

Hazel growled.

"No, no, no," I said. "Quiet, Hazel."

The orange glow flickered in the dark, as if it were moving far away.

Amid the scratching, I could hear quiet breathing. Not just one thing, but many, many things—and then the sounds escaped Hazel's vocal cords before I could stop her.

RAWRK!

RAWRK!

RAW-RAW-RAWRK!

I yelled as fluttering spilled out of the blackness.

Thousands of wings scraped against my skin. There were thousands of bats this time, maybe tens of thousands, but I couldn't see them.

I dragged Hazel to the ground but regretted it. The smell of the bat dung was even stronger.

We had to run for it.

I ran back toward the opening of the cave, but I smacked into a wall.

Where was it? I felt around feverishly for an opening, but there was none. I seized a bat and screamed as it shrieked at me.

My ears rang as I pulled Hazel in the opposite direction, deeper into the abyss as the column of bats whirled around us.

My shoes smashed more bat dung. Hazel kept barking. The bats kept shrieking.

The ground sloped downward and I fell. Hazel rolled ahead of me and I lost her.

"Hazel!"

The bats filled the space between us.

I shielded my face and pushed through the bats, but the shrieking grew louder.

The orange glow pulled at the corner of my vision. It flamed bigger now, but I still couldn't see what it was.

"Hazel, come!" I cried, running forward.

I kept telling her to come, and her bark grew louder.

"Closer, Hazel!" I said, tearing through the bats now.

I yelled as they bore down on me harder, their wings slashing every part of me.

Closer....Closer...Come on, Lester! I wasn't about to be made a punk by a thousand bats!

I shouted Hazel's name as I dove toward the orange light.

The ground sloped deeper and I fell into a roll, bouncing on rock after rock.

The bats subsided, and for a moment, it was just me rolling like a rag doll across the rocks.

I flew off a stone ramp and landed face-first on a stone floor.

I was in some kind of circular chamber. A dozen torches lined the smooth stone walls.

Behind me, an opening to the darkness loomed. Thousands of brown bats poured out of it, circling the ceiling.

Hazel appeared within the column of bats, sliding down the stone ramp. She slid off the ramp and landed next to me.

The last of the bats flew out of the darkness and gathered on the ceiling, hanging upside-down and staring at us. Then they went quiet, crawling over each other. Their entire mass looked like an angry brown sea.

I stood and Hazel brushed against my legs.

"Where are we now?" I asked. "Well, at least we're alive."

The torches crackled and blazed with renewed vigor.

The stone floor shook, and suddenly, it moved downward.

The walls rumbled. Rocks fell from above and I ducked as they crashed to the floor.

An arched door appeared in the wall as the floor stopped. It was tall and skinny, and I had to move sideways to enter.

I emerged into a giant crypt. Wall-to-wall catacombs as far as I could see. Hexagonal slots speckled the walls—I assumed they were crypts.

A voice called my name.

Bo.

Hazel wagged her tail and charged forward into the crypt. Bo appeared in the distance, waving. His purple tracksuit stuck out among the drab crypts.

We ran at each other for what seemed like minutes. From what I could gauge, we had to be a mile apart.

"You won't believe what I just saw," Bo said.

"Bats?" I asked.

"Huh?"

Just before we met, I crashed into something.

I fell backward onto the cold stone floor.

Bo kept running and smacked into a glass wall.

We were separated.

The ground rumbled and the crypt began to revolve. Slowly, Bo disappeared as a wall of tombs covered the glass.

"Bo?" I asked.

Silence.

The torches on the wall crackled again.

Behind us, a wooden dais had appeared out of nowhere. Carpeted steps led up to a wooden coffin. The lid lay propped up against the side of the box.

I gulped.

A cold wind blew me forward and I staggered up the dais.

I didn't want to peek in that coffin, but my feet propelled me forward. Lord God, I didn't want to know what was in there, but I looked.

It was empty.

A cold wind blew, knocking the lid to the ground with a hollow slam.

I jumped.

Then I saw the letters carved into the box.

I stumbled backward, shaking my head.

My name was engraved on the coffin.

CHAPTER NINE

If this were a movie, this would be the part where all the black people in the audience would shout at the screen, saying things like, "Don't get in that coffin!" or "You better not!" or "Man, you crazy!"

Trust me, I was thinking those same things as I stood on the dais.

Me, die tonight? Sheeeeeeet...

But as the cold wind blew me toward the smooth, finished pine wood, I couldn't resist the allure of that coffin. It smelled like juniper with hints of sweetness and rot. Spending eternal rest in a coffin like this would have beat your run-of-the-mill metal casket any day. At one point in a decade or so, you'd be one with the earth; the pine would rot away and worms would get you. Maybe it was an overly romantic way of thinking about it, but you try staring at a coffin with your name on it and you'll get strange thoughts too.

Besides, I had a feeling this dream wouldn't end until I did what the wind was telling me to do.

I swung one leg into the coffin, and in an instant, I was on my back, looking up at the writhing bats on the ceiling.

I did what vampires did in the movies—I crossed my hands over my chest and I closed my eyes.

Would my time come soon? Maybe, but it wouldn't be like this. And it definitely wouldn't be here.

My eyelids felt heavy and I drifted off into deeper sleep.

∼

I awoke to a falling sensation.

I floated downward through reddish-black darkness.

The coffin was far above me now, like I fell through the bottom.

My senses weren't as sharp. The world around me was soup. Sounds moved a few seconds slower. My thoughts didn't spin as fast...

I descended and descended for what seemed like minutes. Out of the gurgling darkness, I heard Bo's voice in the distance.

"Lester."

"Yeah."

"You all right?" Bo asked.

"Just floating."

"Me too," Bo said. "You said you saw a bunch of bats."

"Like last time," I said. "What did you see on your side?"

"A message," Bo said. "It was written in blood on the walls. It said, "Don't open your eyes."

"Really?"

"Your eyes are closed, right?"

"No."

"Close your eyes, Lester," Bo said as his voice faded away.

I called Bo's name, but all I heard was my voice echoing into the blackish-red infinity.

Reluctantly, I closed my eyes.

An aurora of lights shone against my eyelids. Whatever it was, it was bright and evanescent, like the northern lights.

"Lester Broussard," a voice said. I expected it to be large and booming, but it was quiet and soft-spoken. I couldn't place whether it was male or female.

"Who is this?" I asked.

I landed on a stone floor. I didn't move.

"Rise, but do not open your eyes," the voice said. "You must trust what you are about to experience."

"It would help if I knew who you were," I said.

"In due time," the voice said.

"Fair enough."

Opening my eyes was instinct. It took every ounce of my will for me not to do it.

I rose.

"I'm in your hands now," I said.

"Walk forward until we tell you to stop."

I took ten steps forward until a cold wind blew and the voice stopped me. My shoes stopped on the edge of something.

"Where's my friend?" I asked.

"The undead are beneath our grace," the voice said. "We won't waste our time with a zombie."

"Servant," I corrected.

"It doesn't matter."

Man, Bo couldn't get any love tonight.

The lights blazed brighter against my eyelids now, like the northern lights were going berserk.

"We are the collective subconscious of the vampire race," the voice said. "We are made up of every living vampire in the world. We think, act, and dream collectively, though our living selves are not aware."

"I heard rumors that you all were pretty intimate with each other," I said. "But this isn't what I had in mind."

"We have brought you here today to ask for your help, necromancer."

Yep, the night just got even stranger. Maybe if I kept at it, I would win the Powerball.

"Collective soul," I said. "Is that right?"

"We represent all of vampire kind," the voice said. "You are in a dreaming chamber, two consciousnesses deep. You are the first necromancer to be called here. Treat it as the honor it truly is."

"You and I have different definitions of honor," I said. "If you are who you say you are, why are you talking to me? Vampires and necromancers are enemies. Aren't we breaking some kind of unwritten rule or something?"

"We have no other choice," the voice said sadly. "Lester, the vampire race is in grave danger."

"Let me guess: it has something to do with Fiona," I said.

"She is a renegade who has eschewed our traditions," the voice said. "She should have never been turned into one of us."

"You're upset that she's trying to make you irrelevant?" I asked. "She gets turned, hates her new life so much that she would bend the universe to change it?"

Silence.

"And you don't see a problem with that?" I asked. "Have you ever stopped to think that her feelings are justified?"

"She threatens to rip the very fabric of our existence," the voice said. "She must be stopped."

"It sounds like a problem between vampires," I said. "I don't get involved with existential crises of anyone other than myself. Trust me, I already need a therapist."

The bite mark on my arm pulsed and I grimaced. I gripped my arm, but it didn't help.

"This conflict cannot be solved between vampires," the voice said. "It requires the intermediation of a third party."

"Says who?"

"Says the collective will of our race," the voice said. "The supernatural world is no different from a natural ecosystem. Every being has its place."

I shuddered at the thought of vampires having an actual, legitimate reason to exist. I didn't buy it.

"Without your help, we will collectively die if Fiona succeeds," the voice said. "Fiona will destroy us, and generations of rich legacy will disappear."

"I sympathize," I said. "But I should be going now."

"We predicted that you would resist our plea. Therefore, we will compel your compliance."

The bite mark flared. I yelled as the pain brought me to the floor. Buzz saws might as well have been digging into my wrist a centimeter at a time.

"We have infected you," the voice said. "You are not a vampire, but our blood has mixed with yours. Therefore, if we perish as a race, so will anything that is associated with our kind."

"Including me," I said sarcastically.

"Including you," the voice said.

CHAPTER TEN

In the supernatural world, there's an acronym that I'm not fond of: TANSTAARWOS. And no, it's not a planet from *Star Wars*.

It means "there ain't no such thing as a rendezvous without strings." Whenever two supernatural beings meet on uneven terms, one of them gets screwed. Boy, did I feel like I was getting bent over now.

"You cursed me," I told the voice. "Why didn't I see that coming?"

"Save us, necromancer, and we just might owe you an honest favor," the voice said, drifting away. "Wake up and open your eyes, Lester."

Something catapulted me upward through the bloody darkness.

I opened my eyes.

Warm, humid air filled my lungs.

Ant'ny's face hovered over mine. His voice was distant at first. He shook me.

"Lester, dawg, wake up!"

I bolted up. In the grass next to me, Hazel stirred and opened her eyes.

Ant'ny shook me again.

"Y'all are killin' me, man!" he said. "I can't even go to the bathroom without you pulling something on me."

Bo emerged from the restaurant rubbing his neck with one hand. He carried a bag of food in the other.

"You all right, boss man?" he asked.

"I've been better," I said as Ant'ny helped me up. I felt like I took a long nap. I stretched, popping my legs in their sockets. "How long were we asleep?"

"Just a few minutes," Ant'ny said.

"That sounds about right," I said, yawning.

It sure felt like we were in that dream for much longer than that.

"Let's get out of here," I said, helping Hazel into the car door. She wobbled her way into the backseat.

In the restaurant, a female cashier was staring at us like we were crazy. I couldn't imagine what she was thinking. I waved at her as if to say, "We're all right. Don't worry about us."

I sidestepped out of earshot from Ant'ny and whispered to Bo, "Did you dream about—"

"Vampires," Bo said.

I hung my head for a moment.

"I was hoping all of this *was* a dream," I said.

A loud engine like a giant mosquito buzzed down the street. As it grew louder, the bite mark on my wrist blazed and searing pain ran up my arm.

I looked over just in time to see a lime-green sport motorcycle jump the curb into the parking lot. The driver—in a checkered racing jacket and black visored helmet—pulled a gun from his waist.

Bo pushed me down.

Ant'ny dove into the car and covered his head.

Tap. Tap. Tap.

Bullets hit my fender. Gunsmoke swept across the parking lot.

Tap.

My ears rang so bad, I couldn't even hear my voice.

Tap. Tap. Tap tap tap.

I rolled over and covered my head, coughing on gunsmoke. Thank God the only thing between me and the shooter was the front end of my car.

Bo climbed into the car and opened the glove box, grabbing a pistol.

Tap. Tap.

Bo cranked down the window, and he jumped up and fired a few shots.

Tap. Tap.

One of the bullets struck the bike's chassis. The biker yelled as the blow nearly knocked him off.

He leaned forward and sped out of the parking lot, weaving into traffic. A bundle of twisted locks bounced on the back of his head under his helmet.

Bo dragged me up.

"Let's roll!" he yelled.

Bo burned out of the lot and into traffic in the opposite direction of the bike.

"Home, now!" I said.

Just like last time, we rode all the way home with our eyes in the rearview mirror, and in silence.

CHAPTER ELEVEN

When you return home after a long night's drama, all you want to do is go inside and sit down for a minute.

I did. Bo did. Hazel did—at least I *think* she did.

Ant'ny just wanted to eat his chicken dinner and chocolate cake in peace after all we put him through. I didn't blame him.

The sun sank into the clouds and the last rays of sunlight finally gave way to night as we entered my neighborhood. It was a quiet, wavy cloud, navy sky kind of night, the kind when I loved driving down the boulevards with the windows down, listening to jazz and musing about the world.

After getting shot at, putting my windows down was a bad idea, so I settled for crisp air conditioning.

As Bo eased into the gravel alley behind my house, the headlights illuminated a black sedan parked in front of my garage.

A man stepped out. Young white guy, curly black hair. He wore a black suit with a dark tie and a white shirt. He squinted in the headlights, motioned us to stop.

Bo's hand moved for the gun in the glovebox, but I smacked it away.

"Don't even think about it," I said.

Bo slowed to a stop. He sprang out of the car. I followed.

"Yo, don't you see the garage right there, man?" Bo said.

"Which one of you is Mr. Broussard?" he asked.

"That would be me," I said cautiously.

The man flashed a gold badge.

"You said you'd be home at five o'clock and not to worry," he said, frowning. "It's six, Mr. Broussard."

Shit. My night had been bad enough. I forgot all about the detective.

"Damian Harris, STLPD," he said.

I sighed. "I'm sorry, Detective Harris. I didn't intend to miss our meeting, but I've been through hell tonight."

"We got a report of a tan Lincoln Town Car that was involved in a shooting about fifteen minutes ago," Harris said. "Was that you?"

"I know I've wasted your time," I said. "How much more you got?"

"All night," he said, putting his hands on his hips.

"Then come on," I said. "I'll tell you everything you want to know."

Harris moved his car so we could get into my detached garage. As Bo put the car in park, I turned to Ant'ny.

"I appreciate everything you helped us with today," I said. "But if I were you, I'd go home—expeditiously."

"Ain't gotta tell me twice," Ant'ny said, grabbing his bucket of fried chicken. "I'm eating my dinner, taking a shower, and praying at my bedside after all you put me through."

"Pray for me," I said. "Gotta feeling I'm gonna need it."

"Throw in a few good words for me while you're at it, bruh," Bo said, grinning an ugly smile.

I entered my backyard and let Harris in through the gate.

"This is my neighbor, Anthony," I said as I clanged the gate shut.

"Sup, Detective," Ant'ny said, saluting. Harris nodded. Ant'ny skipped ahead and quickly disappeared into the gangway. The last thing my neighbor needed was a run-in with the police.

Bo, Harris, Hazel, and I walked through my backyard bathed in starlight. My house was dark. I usually left a light on or two—it was good security. I hadn't expected to be away for so long.

"Since when did the STLPD have a paranormal crimes division?" I asked.

"We formed a couple of years back," Harris said, looking around the yard. He was looking for threats. "There have been growing supernatural disturbances in the city. Of course, the public doesn't know we exist."

I unlocked my back door and turned on the porch light, flooding the backyard with a warm light that made a rabbit burst from under my porch and into the grass.

Inside, I led Harris to the kitchen and pulled out a chair for him. Hazel grazed at her food bowl and settled into her bed in the corner of the kitchen by the radiator.

Bo plopped down at the kitchen table and rubbed his neck.

"I'd offer you something, but I assume you won't take it," I said, pulling a beer from the refrigerator.

"Correct," Harris said, hesitating a moment. "Is there anyone else in the house?"

"Just us," I said, cracking my tab. "I'd know if we had intruders."

That reminded me to pick up some extra crickets at the pet shop for the spider on my porch door. The little guy had been through a lot after the bat attack.

Seeing the kitchen safe, Harris pulled up a chair at the table. Then I noticed that he was carrying a leather portfolio.

To say this guy was young was an understatement. He had to be in his thirties. A couple of days' old stubble covered up his baby face. He wasn't stocky, but muscular, like you'd expect from a cop early in his career. The way he walked, he was used to the hood. This must have been his territory, and that was saying something. Heaven help and God bless the police who took regular assignments in my neighborhood. But the real truth was that he probably had the gentrified parts too. A lot of white people were moving to my neighborhood from the suburbs wanting the city living experience, and they were snatching up the abandoned lots for pennies on the dollar. In a few more years, black folks might be a rare sight.

"First things first," Harris said, sitting the portfolio on the table. "If you two were in real trouble, you would have been in handcuffs by now."

"Comforting," Bo said. "I guess now's not the time to tell you about that bank we robbed."

Harris stared at him.

"Bo, shut up," I said.

"I, uh, guess that wasn't very funny," Bo said. "My bad. We didn't rob any banks, man."

Harris opened the portfolio and pulled out a manila folder.

"Again, I preface our conversation with the fact that you two aren't in trouble," he said, pulling several photographs out of the folder and sliding them over to me, "because these photographs may freak you out. But I'm not after you. I'm after the truth."

The photos were of me.

Security camera surveillance by the looks of it. Me in my gabardine by the river front. I was running.

I recognized it—it was from the same footage that Fiona showed me. At the riverfront running from a gang of jinn.

Another photo was of me at a blackjack table in the casino. Again, similar to the photos Fiona showed me in her video.

"I was assigned to an incident report that the regular PD

couldn't figure out," Harris said. "A couple of weeks ago, we received a report of a fight and chase through the casino floor. Shortly after, the fight picked up at the riverfront. Security footage placed you there."

"Yeah, it was me," I said.

"What happened?" Harris asked.

At this point, I had to make a choice: tell the detective everything and risk getting slapped with some kind of charge, or hope that he was reasonable enough to understand what was going on and listen to me without judging. From what I knew about detectives, they never asked a question they didn't know the answer to. Given all I'd been through so far, you can understand why I was cautious.

"I was celebrating my birthday, Detective," I said.

Harris grinned. "You sure know how to party."

"Ain't that the truth," I said. "I didn't go looking for a fight. An old friend needed my help."

"That corroborates my findings, so thank you," Harris said. "You see, I did some digging, and I found out about you and the demon Visgaroth."

Bo's eyes widened. "How do you know about that?"

"I have my sources," Harris said. "Anyway, I've got you at the casino in the middle of a fight, at the riverfront, and again at the Arch. I don't know what Visgaroth did to you, but I for one am grateful he's gone."

I didn't expect him to say that.

"Visgaroth made shadow deals with certain folks across the city," Harris said. "We were monitoring them for criminal behavior. His untimely death stopped any future evil."

"You have no idea how correct you are," I said.

"That's a long preamble to the real reason I'm here," Harris said, producing more evidence from his envelope. One was a photograph of Fiona, stylish as ever in her ruby red beret, pink sweater, and gigantic sunglasses. She was walking with an entourage of her vampires—looked like they were in a shopping mall of some kind.

"I've been tracking this woman for the last few months," Harris said. "Her name is Fiona. I haven't been able to discover a last name. I have reason to believe she's a—"

"Vampire," I said.

Harris stopped. "What do you know?"

"I'll tell you when you finish," I said.

"Well, about five people in leadership positions at the casino and hotel went missing a few months ago," Harris said. "It's the single biggest unsolved missing person case in the city, and we're keeping it out of the press as long as we can. That's where I come in."

"So the people missing got turned into vampires, huh?" Bo asked. "That's cold, man."

"We think Fiona targeted the leaders so she could take over the casino," Harris said. "We've seen her coming in and out of the executive suites every day. From the looks of her, she's in charge."

"She is," I said.

"Have you met her?" Harris asked.

"I just had the pleasure," I said, taking a big chug of my beer. It was bitter, like my feelings. "It's why I was late."

"I'm glad I found you, then," Harris said.

"Before we continue," I said, "you have to understand that I'm a little cautious about talking to police about the supernatural."

Harris leaned back in his chair. "I'd be cautious too."

He pulled a detective pad and pen out of his portfolio and clicked his pen.

"I need your help in investigating Fiona," Harris said. "We're talking about the lives of five people here, and worse."

"What do you want from me?" I asked.

"What can you tell me about Fiona?" Harris asked.

"It's worse than you think," I said. "You're on a missing

person case, but it's deeper than that. She's threatening to destroy the entire vampire race."

Harris scribbled something. "Is that a bad thing?"

"That was my first thought," I said, "but there's more to the story. I just don't know it yet."

"Yeah, Fiona and her posse of millennial vampires want to take over the world with driverless cars," Bo said.

"Blue hatchbacks?" Harris asked. "I'm aware of those."

"The vampire race is running scared," I said. "They're not pleased with her prospects."

"What exactly is she trying to do?" Harris asked.

"She has an aversion to blood," I said. "And apparently doesn't like being a child of the night. She wants to change that by destroying her desire for blood with a cure for vampirism."

Harris screwed up his face.

I didn't like being an ambassador for Fiona's diabolical plans, but somebody had to tell him.

"You can't be serious," Harris said. "That's not even possible...is it?"

"She's done a couple of shadow deals, so anything is possible," I said.

"Why did she call you?" Harris asked.

"She asked me to stay home and sit idly by while she executes her plans. She knows I'm a threat."

"Uh-huh," Harris said. He wrote something down, pondered for a moment, and said, "*Are* you going to stay home and watch?"

"My only choice is to fight, Detective," I said. "I don't know how to do anything else at this point. I get the feeling that staying home is a bad idea."

Fiona's words ran through my mind again: "If you meddle in my affairs, you're avocado toast, Lester." And then I remembered the Vampire Collective: "Our blood has mixed with yours. Therefore, if we perish at midnight, so will anything that is associated with our kind...including you."

Was there any way I could win?

My favorite card game is blackjack. Sometimes when you're playing it, you're close to the limit—twenty-one—and everything depends on the next card you draw. There are no absolutes. You either win or bust. At this point, I had a hand worth seventeen and the chances were very high that my next move would put me over twenty-one. If this were a card game, I'd stand all day long and hope for the best. That is, unless I was willing to cheat.

"I'm here because I need a lead," Harris said. "I need information on what happened to the missing people. And if what you're saying is true, I need help in stopping Fiona."

"I wish I could help you with the missing folks," I said, "but that's not—"

"Your area," Harris said, finishing my thought. "This is a favor. You're the only one who can help me."

"I've heard that before," I said, rising.

"I need your necromancy," Harris said.

"Be careful what you wish for," Bo said. "Nothing good comes from talking to the dead. Ain't that right, Lester?"

I nodded. "I don't think our dear detective can be persuaded, can he?"

Harris shook his head. "We don't have much time."

I stared at him for a moment.

"I can't seem to get any information," Harris said. "All I'm asking for are a few clues."

"Isn't that cheating?" Bo asked. "Don't courts have rules against evidence gathered unfairly or something like that?"

"All's fair in love, war, and the supernatural, and I have a feeling this won't go to court," I said, opening the door to my basement. "Okay, Detective Harris. I'll do you a favor. I reserve the right to cash your favor out however I choose—legally, of course."

"Deal," Harris said, rising.

Bo smacked his head. "Here we go again. I'll get the chalk..."

He jogged downstairs.

"Follow me to the dungeon," I said, grinning.

CHAPTER TWELVE

Unlike most things in the supernatural, necromancy is subtle. When you think *supernatural*, the last thing you probably think of is necromancy. That's by design.

Vampirism is a shriek—it's all show, fangs, and blood. Vampires are quick to throw their power around.

Necromancy is a whisper. A necromancer doesn't need very much to use their power, and a little bit goes a long way. Our strength doesn't come from powers like super strength or immortality. It comes from the power of suggestion, and a precious resource—the dead. Without their cooperation, we can't accomplish anything. So I suppose you could say we're smooth talkers and fast persuaders.

My good friend, CeCe, used to call me Lester "Tongues" Broussard back in the day. She said I could talk the dead into doing damn near anything. That's not entirely true, but it is a skill set. Many wannabe necromancers have died over the years because they didn't have the verbal skills needed to work with spirits.

The dead aren't like you and me. They *were* like us before they died, but their reality is forever warped once they pass. It's like becoming an adult, losing your virginity, or having major surgery—your perspective on life isn't the same afterward. *Their* perspective no longer includes time.

They suddenly know everything that has been, is, and will be. It's a terrible burden, and it takes eons to adjust to it. Some can't make sense of it and become confused at what they see. That's why obtaining information from the dead can be a fool's errand.

Demons are more reliable. They don't suffer from the perspective problem and you can persuade them with blood. The only downside is they will feed you misinformation if they sense weakness, so you have to have a good bullshit filter. See why I said good interpersonal skills are a requirement for this job?

I wondered if Harris knew what he was getting himself into as Bo and I prepped my basement for a calling.

I had cleaned up my basement after my last adventure, and it was looking mighty fine tonight. I kept the place even cleaner than usual, though I couldn't get the mildew smell out. I had ranged all my boxes of memories along the walls and sealed them. Last time, a photograph slipped out of one of the boxes during a rendezvous with a demon, and it created a headache for me.

I bought a cheap white storage cabinet from a local thrift store and used it to organize and store all of my necromancy tools: children's chalk, balls of yarn, unscented candles, blankets, wooden bowls, a broom, a dustpan, and salt. Yes, sir, this cabinet was my toolbox, and I couldn't help but smile as I opened it up to see all my things hanging from hooks and ordered on shelves—exactly where they should have been.

I grabbed a broom and swept the floor vigorously.

Bo grabbed some chalk and followed me by drawing an inner circle on the concrete floor, then a bigger, outer circle. I'd finally trained him to draw proper circles.

Harris inspected my cabinet.

"This is *all* you use?" he asked, incredulous.

"What were you expecting?" I asked. "A goat sacrifice?"

"That's always how I learned," Harris said.

I stopped sweeping. "What else did you expect?" I asked.

"You make it look simple, that's all," Harris said, shrugging. "Maybe that's why I couldn't get anywhere. I was making it too complicated."

"So you're a necromancer," I said, laughing. "The plot thickens, doesn't it, Bo?"

"I thought Lester was the only one using his powers for good," Bo said. "I'll be damned."

"No wonder why you're in the Paranormal Crimes Division, Detective," I said, finishing my sweep.

Bo drew a pentagram in the inner circle. I threw a blanket into the inner circle and put a bowl of salt on it. Bo lit several candles and placed them around the circle.

"Tell me something, Detective," I said. "You said you couldn't find any leads. I'm guessing you tried to summon the dead?"

"Several times," he said. "But I couldn't find anyone who would give me reliable information."

"How long have you practiced the dark arts?" I asked.

"About a year," he said.

"Jesus," I said. "They say if you survive your first year, your chances of not getting killed go up dramatically. Congratulations."

The good news was that I could trust Harris. Normally, necromancers gave off creepy vibes.

No necromancer in their right mind would ever be a detective. First off, possessing a dead body is illegal. Second, think about all the murders you could find the killers for, but have no evidence to prove it. Solve too few murders and you'd never be able to sleep because you'd know who the killers were. Solve too many murders and you'd attract unwanted scrutiny. It'd drive any righteous person nuts. No, most necros stayed in the shadows, in funeral homes, or science laboratories, where their desire for cadavers would've been more likely to be unnoticed.

I liked that Harris narrowed his focus to the supernatural rather than regular murders. That showed restraint.

"Who are we summoning?" Harris asked as I flicked off the lights.

"You haven't been able to find a lead because you don't have a reputation yet," I said. "I'm calling someone I can trust."

"CeCe?" Bo asked.

"No, I love her to death, but I don't feel like owing a lich a favor tonight."

"Jesus, you're friends with a lich?" Harris asked.

"I'll tell you about it sometime," I said. "But I'm not calling a lich tonight. I'm calling one of the only souls in the afterlife that I can trust, the smartest person I knew here among the living, and someone who will tell me the truth—no bullshit."

"Oh, your son, Marcus," Bo said, nodding with approval. "Smart. Real smart. I liked him."

"No," I said as we sat down on the blanket. I smiled and closed my eyes. "Gentlemen, I'm calling my dead wife."

CHAPTER THIRTEEN

"I FINALLY GET to meet the pretty lady I've heard so much about," Bo said. "This is gonna be a real pleasure, Lester."

I laughed. It was a real pleasure for me too.

For seven years, I swore off necromancy and said that I would never touch the dark arts again.

My wife, Amira, or Am as I called her, made the ultimate sacrifice, one I did not ask her to make.

She was the reason I became a necromancer. Have you ever loved someone so much that even the thought of losing them struck your heart out?

Amira was my second wife and the only person who made me believe in love. When we got her second cancer diagnosis, I cursed the world. I cursed God. I said, "Not in my house." Most people would have read up on science and cancer treatments. I swore that I would bend the universe around me to protect my family.

I sought out black magic. You know the rest.

But never in a million years did I ever expect my wife to be the price I would pay.

You know the funny thing?

During my seven-year solitude, I could have called Amira

any time to say I was sorry. But I was so ashamed. I couldn't bring myself to talk to her until a few weeks ago, after I killed Visgaroth. And true to her spirit, she forgave me before I could even say a word.

"Don't apologize," she said. She told me that all was well, and that I wouldn't believe all the things she's seen. She had moved on.

I cried like a baby. She told me to cheer up, and to use my magic to do some good in the little time I had left. We've talked a few times since then.

I lost my wife and son to death, and my daughter to estrangement. All these years, I've been trying to figure out how to live with a quarter of my heart. Three-fourths of it was broken.

Love hard, grieve hard—you just gotta keep livin', I guess.

As we sat on the blanket, I closed my eyes and said, "Amira Broussard, I send out a beacon of light to you to ask for your help. Please stop and offer your assistance."

We waited.

Usually, calling the dead is like fishing for spirits. If you don't have a name, you don't know who is liable to show up in your circle. But because I had my wife's name, and because everything in the basement was half hers, it was easy to attract her.

I said the incantation again: "Amira Broussard, I send out a beacon of light to you to ask for your help. Please stop and offer your assistance."

Then I whispered, "Am, I really need to talk to you."

My furnace whooshed on and the ducts over our heads rattled.

My wife's voice spoke, barely audible. I knew her breathy voice anywhere.

"Lester."

"Baby," I said, not opening my eyes. "I'm so glad to hear your voice."

"Lester, honey."

"I hear you."

"I need you...to listen."

"I'm listening."

Something nudged me.

"Yo, uh, Lester," Bo said.

"Not now, Bo," I said angrily.

"Eyes open, Lester," Harris said.

I opened my eyes to a giant human-grasshopper hybrid hanging from a silver thread on the ceiling. Human hands held on to the string, grown from its back like a horrific lab experiment. He stared at me with red-jeweled eyes, and a mouth full of saw teeth. His wings rested against its back. He hung over the outer circle.

"Lester," the demon said, mimicking my wife's voice. "Baby, it's not safe for you to summon spirits in your condition."

The demon abruptly changed to a harsh, grating voice that sounded like a droning fly mixed with a high school geek's.

"Natkaal," I said. "I didn't call you."

"Consider me a proxy," the demon said. "Did you seriously think that you could summon a spirit?"

"Get the hell out of my home," I said.

The last time I spoke with Natkaal, I had to broker a shadow deal. It was a pain in the ass. I wanted my wife.

"I can't leave—not yet, Lester," the demon said. His human hands tugged in the silver thread. The demon expanded his mosaicked wings, and every vein on them shimmered in the candlelight. "I was told to deliver you a message: you are forbidden from calling spirits until further notice. Of course, I hate to be the one to tell you this. I'm a mere demon, and who am I to be trusted? But when the Lich King gives you an order, you obey. You can't imagine the favors he owes me now—"

"The Lich King sent you?" I asked. "Prove it."

Halgeron the Lich King and I weren't on good terms. It didn't surprise me that he wanted to ban me from the spirit world, but I didn't know why.

"If you don't believe me, there's nothing I can say that will change your mind," Natkaal said impetuously. "But don't forget that I kept my promise to you last time, necromancer. You shouldn't mistrust my credibility."

It *was* true that Natkaal upheld his part of the deal last time. But demons don't have track records. Everything they do is self-serving, even if you don't know the motive.

"Let's say you're telling the truth," Bo said. "Why did Lester get banned?"

"That's the most exciting part," Natkaal said, flashing a devilish grin. "She can't speak to one whose soul isn't intact. Hmm, maybe that bite mark is deeper than you think..."

I cursed.

Vampires can't enter the afterlife because they don't have souls. Those goddamned vampires not only infected my blood, but they must also have infected my soul too.

"Of course," the demon continued, "it's not possible for you to speak with Amira, per se. But I suppose I could bend the supernatural continuum and create a projection of her so that you can be reunited with your beautiful wife..."

"You know what?" I asked, smiling. "I think I'm going to bend the supernatural continuum right now by kicking you out of my house. I'm not doing any shadow deals tonight. Get out, and good riddance."

Natkaal's face turned sour. "You need me more than I need you."

"We'll see about that," I said. "Be gone, and do not return unless I will you."

Natkaal screamed.

"You'll come begging to me before long, Lester. You're a heathen just like the rest of us!"

I snuffed out the candles and threw a pinch of salt at the demon. It faded away and the furnace died. Silence swept across the basement as the demon's screams dissipated.

"That's not what I expected," Harris said.

"Me either," I said. "Detective, I've been screwed."

"More like bitten," Bo said.

"So you can't communicate with the dead at all unless you pay off that demon?" Harris asked. "Damn it. You were my ace in the hole, Mr. Broussard."

"I'm not finished yet," I said. "If there's one thing I've learned over the years, it's never to trust a demon."

"You're just a baby necro, Harris," Bo said. "I hope you don't ever have to learn that lesson the hard way."

"I've learned much harder lessons than that on the police force, trust me," Harris said, springing up. "Gentlemen, I appreciate your time."

"No, no," I said. "I'm not done yet."

I grabbed a razor blade from my cabinet and made a small cut on my palm. I squeezed out a few drops of blood into the floor—my offering to the spirit world. I focused my thoughts on the afterlife, making my intent to enter the only thing on my mind.

Here's what should have happened next: a hole glimpsing into the spirit world should have opened up in the air next to me, and I should have been able to grab at the edges and pull myself through. I did this countless times and it was like second nature to me.

What actually happened: nothing. Blue sparks flew up in front of my face, like a lighter that wouldn't start.

Then I felt a cold point of metal on my throat. A woman's shadow stood in front of me, a rose-gold sword leveled at my Adam's apple.

"Stop right there."

I knew the voice. I knew the shape of the woman.

"CeCe, what are you doing?" I asked.

Silence.

CeCe, my dear old friend, and a lich. She and I had been necromancers together back in the day, and I called on her from time to time for help. Her job: warden of the dead.

"I can't let you continue," she said.

I missed her vibrancy—stark, flowing red dress, pale skin, cadaverous smile. Instead, it looked like someone had dimmed all the colors on her body to a staticky monochrome. I couldn't even see her face.

"I'm sorry," she said. "but Natkaal was right."

My heart sank.

"You have been infected," CeCe said. "Your soul is stained, and I can no longer permit you to enter the spirit world."

CHAPTER FOURTEEN

I was locked out of the spirit world when I needed it the most. My night just kept getting worse.

"Lester can't enter because his soul is stained?" Bo asked. "You ain't exactly pure either, sis."

CeCe lowered her sword. "But at least my soul is not stained. It's supernatural law. I can't change it."

Harris shook his head. "I got a lot more trouble than what I expected today."

I grabbed his shoulder. "I'm not done yet. I've got as much stake in this as you do. Don't give up on me."

He nodded.

I sat down on my steps. CeCe sat next to me. We didn't say anything for a few moments. I couldn't get over the absence of color in her body, like she was planets away, even though she was sitting next to me. Sometimes I couldn't believe that a good friend of mine was a lich. Few necromancers had this honor, and here I was, unable to take advantage of it.

"I'm in real trouble, aren't I, CeCe?" I asked.

"This is worse than last time," she said, "and I wasn't sure it could get much worse. I can't help you this time. Halgeron has prevented me from getting involved. I should have already left."

"I wasn't going to ask for help," I said, "but it would have been nice to ask Amira for assistance."

"You'll have to do things the hard way," she said. "The only bright side I see is that Bo was also stained, so you can continue to use him as your servant."

"Help me understand this collective vampire consciousness," I said.

CeCe shrugged. "Vampires are outside my jurisdiction. Anything goes with them. What did you see?"

"I spoke to something and it told me it was the collective consciousness of every vampire in the world," I said. "It infected my blood so that I would do its bidding. Problem is, I don't disagree with what they asked me to do. But if I fail, I die along with them."

"In which case, you turn to dust," CeCe said.

"Apparently."

"Hmm," CeCe said. "If it were me, I'd consider a shadow deal."

"I knew you were going to tell me that," I said. "That damned demon was right."

CeCe began to fade away. "I'm sorry, Lester. I can't do much more for you."

I hated to see her go. My only link to the spirit world was completely severed now.

But damn it, I wasn't going to get played by a demon.

"Harris, I have another idea," I said, staring at him. The long stare made him uncomfortable. The detective didn't get the hint.

Bo gave a knowing nod. "Here's what we need you to do," he said. "Go to the spirit world. Chat with Amira for a minute, and then bring back the info to us. Ain't that right, boss man?"

"You up to it?" I asked.

Harris looked like he was going to be sick.

"I've never been to the spirit world," he said.

"You truly are a baby necro, then," Bo said. "Isn't that an essential skill?"

"Think you can try?" I asked.

Harris shook his head. "I'm not going there. I may never come back. I only use necromancy for information—I'm not interested in...the rest."

"Aside from the threat of demons, errant spirits, sword-wielding liches, and a big-ass Lich King the size of a football field, what could go wrong?" Bo asked, grinning.

"If you have any reservations, it might be too risky," I said. "I can walk you through exactly what to do. All we need you to do is get some information—if you're willing."

Harris sighed.

"This could be the lead you've been looking for," I said.

Harris braced the wall and said, "All right, you win. Tell me what I have to do."

I sanitized my razor blade in a nearby sink and handed it to him.

"You're looking pale," I said.

He didn't look pale. But I wanted to goad him a little so I could make sure he could do it.

"I've got it," he said, staring at the razor blade.

"You sure, man?" Bo asked. "If you're gonna fall out, now's the time."

Harris took a deep sigh. "I'm a police officer. Why the hell am I scared of this?"

"Fear is natural," I said. "I'd be more worried if you weren't scared."

"What do they teach you at the academy?" Bo asked. "Don't they do role plays or something? You know, poster board criminals that pop out of closets? Imagine that."

"It's nothing like this," he said.

"No, don't listen to Bo," I said, giving him the side-eye.

"Detective Harris, the first thing I want you to do is imagine the afterlife."

"Does it...look a certain way?" Harris asked.

"That doesn't matter," I said. "What matters is your intent. Imagine it with all your being. Will the image to the front of your mind—make it so vivid as if you were there. Feel the air on your face. See spirits circling the air. The only thing I want you to think about is entering this place. You have to want it more than anything you've ever wanted in your life. You have to imagine that this place is the solution to all your problems."

I pretended to make a slashing motion in the center of my palm. "Then, cut."

"Cut," Harris said quietly.

I grabbed a silver necklace from the cabinet—one of my wife's favorite pieces of jewelry. "When you get to the spirit world, hold this in your hand and call Amira."

I stepped back and folded my arms as Harris closed his eyes and inhaled another deep breath. He took his time.

Then he raised the razor blade to his palm, eyes still closed, and he cut his wrist. But the cut wasn't hard enough.

Bo winced as Harris dug the blade into his skin again, this time drawing a thin line of blood. He didn't flinch.

A gust ripped across the room, forcing Harris's eyes open.

A jagged stitch of blue light hovered in front of Harris. The dark valleys of the spirit world lay ahead, muddled by haze.

"My God," Harris said.

"You're in control, Detective Harris," I said. "You're only there for one reason. Get out once you've got the information."

Harris jumped into the portal to the spirit world and it zipped shut after him.

"Welp, he did it," Bo said. "I didn't think he was gonna do it."

"Me either," I said. "Now, we wait."

Bo and I cleaned up the floor from our summoning session. It took approximately two minutes. I know because I put on one of my jazz records on my turntable, and the first song is about two minutes.

Just as the song was ending, a hole to the spirit world appeared and Harris flew out amid clods of dirt and crashed into a stack of cardboard boxes. Dirt rained across the floor.

A demonic scream stopped me cold as a giant insect face with a mouth full of saw teeth pushed against the hole, bristling and shifting like a living pin art design with iron filings.

"Lester Broussard, you bastard!" the voice cried.

Natkaal.

"I told you the truth!" the demon said. "And if you want to talk to your sweet wife, you go through *me*, got it?"

"Go to hell," I said.

"It's a shadow deal or nothing if you want your wife," the demon said, growling. "Try to circumvent me again, and I'll destroy innocent people in your name. How does that sound, necromancer?"

The demon roared and the portal disappeared.

I stared at the place where the portal had been, balling my fists. No demon was going to keep me from my wife. I might have been a lot of things tonight, but I sure as heck wasn't going to be some demon's punk. If he wanted to boss me around, he should have taken a number.

"At least your face is intact, Harris," Bo said, helping Harris up.

Harris felt his face in horror. Then he shook his head.

"So much for a lead," he said.

"What happened?" I asked.

"As soon as I entered the spirit world, I did what you told me—after I got over the initial shock of being there," Harris said. "As soon as I called Amira's name, the demon came out of nowhere and crashed into me."

"He's hellbent on a shadow deal," I said. "I'm not going to do it."

Bo scratched his head. "But we need his help."

"Tanstaarwos," I said.

"Tansta what?" Bo asked, screwing up his face.

"It means there ain't no such thing as a rendezvous without strings," I said. "If I did a deal with Natkaal now, chances are I'd get screwed somehow."

"If you haven't noticed, we're kind of screwed already," Bo said.

"Never do a deal when it comes out of nowhere," I said. "It's almost always a trap. You wouldn't take out a home loan from a random company that robo-dialed your number, would you?"

"True," Bo said. "You're spittin' that wisdom like always, man."

"What now?" Harris asked.

I was about to tell Harris how I needed time to think, when I heard footsteps just outside my basement window. Sounded like shoes on gravel. A shadow lurched past the window, elongated against my curtains.

Bo and Harris saw it too.

"Someone's outside," I whispered, my senses heightening.

Bo flew to the basement door and opened it.

"Hey!" he yelled into the backyard.

Harris drew his gun and followed as Bo scrambled up the stairs underneath my back porch.

A voice shouted, "Yo, don't! Stop!"

Outside, Bo pounced on a shadow and held it down. Harris aimed his gun at a black man in a red hoodie on the ground.

"It's me," the man said, pulling back his hood. "Don't shoot!"

Bo cocked his head. "Ant'ny?"

"Y'all are crazy, I'm tellin' you!" Ant'ny said.

"You the crazy one," Bo said, getting off.

"I wanted to figure out what the hell y'all were doing," he said. "You were acting funny."

I cursed under my breath as I walked up the stairs and into my backyard. Ant'ny had never left my property. He probably hung out in the gangway until we were in the house, then snuck to the windows to watch us. That explained why my spiders didn't alert me—they know him.

"Why were you all in a circle?" Ant'ny asked. "I couldn't see much through the curtains, but—"

"Stop talking," Bo said. "You're moving into dangerous territory."

"I'm already in it," Ant'ny said.

"We were singing hymns and giving thanks to the good Lord," Bo said. "You happy? Now go home, man."

"Hymns my foot," Ant'ny said. "I ain't seen neither of you go to church. Let me guess, did the detective lead the prayer?"

Harris tucked his gun in his holster. "So he doesn't know, Lester?"

"Not a thing," I whispered. "I had hoped to keep it that way."

"Know what?" Ant'ny asked.

"Cat's out of the bagel now," Bo said.

Ant'ny pushed Bo away and rested on the ground. "I feel like I got hit by a house."

"I'll take that as a compliment," Bo said, grinning.

"So which one of y'all is gonna start talkin'?" Ant'ny asked.

"Nobody," I said. "Please go home, Ant'ny."

He stared at me.

"Ant'ny," I said, "remember when you were a kid, and you and your sister used to come around here, and I told you those Mafia jokes?"

He nodded.

"What did I say?" I asked.

"If I told you, I'd have to kill you," Ant'ny said with an Italian accent. "So you're threatening me, eh, wise guy?"

"I wouldn't dream of it," I said. "But if you keep hanging around us, somebody's gonna get hurt, and it could be you."

I entered the gangway and held open the gate. "It's not you; it's us."

Ant'ny looked at Bo, Harris, and then me before shaking his head. He threw up his hands and stood.

Have you ever had one of those moments when your brain tells you, "Shut up and stay quiet and you just may get out of this without a headache?" I heard it and I listened. And then Bo had to go and open his mouth.

"I guess I'll be the neighborhood dummy," Ant'ny said. "Too stupid know anything. Just tell old Ant'ny to shuffle along and mind his own business. Y'all are cold."

"Go home," Bo said. "You don't want a red pill moment tonight, dog."

My jaw dropped.

If there was one thing you didn't do with Ant'ny, it was insult his intelligence. You had to let him down gently. I think it had something to do with his time in prison. *He* could call himself a fool all day long, but if you did…

"What do you mean red pill?" Ant'ny asked.

"Go home," Bo said.

"Ant'ny, Bo is an idiot," I said. "You know that as well as I do."

Bo rubbed the back of his head.

"What's the red pill?" Ant'ny asked, approaching Bo. "Since you brought it up, why don't you tell me?"

Harris stood between them.

"Mr. Rice, this is getting out of hand," Harris said. "I need you to leave because you're impeding official police business."

Ant'ny paused.

"When this is all over, I suggest you talk to Lester and ask him to tell you what's going on," Harris said, "but right now, this conversation isn't productive."

"All right," Ant'ny said. "I'll listen to you, Detective."

And then Ant'ny skirted around Harris and pointed at Bo.

"I'm not stupid, man," he said. "What's the red pill? Huh? Tell me what the damn red pill is!"

Harris grabbed Ant'ny. An explosion threw Ant'ny into the side of my house and he fell to the ground with a crunch.

"Harris, what the hell?" Bo asked.

Harris looked down at his hands in horror. "I didn't do it. I mean, I—"

I ran to Ant'ny. He slumped down, his head against his chest.

I shook him and called his name. Bo and Harris crowded around me.

Ant'ny jerked awake. His eyes had that dazed, just-woke-up-and-don't-know-where-I-am-for-a-second look before they locked on me. Then his gaze wandered to Bo and he screamed.

"Get away from me!"

He pushed me away and tripped into the shadows of the gangway.

"Jesus, what the hell is going on?" he asked.

"Ant'ny, it's us," I said.

He shook his head. "Not you. Not you—"

He pointed to Bo. And then he screamed again, clutching his head as he dropped to the ground.

"What happened?" Harris asked, his voice trembling.

Ant'ny vomited. I patted and rubbed him on the back, told him to take his time.

"Ant'ny," I said softly. "What's going on?"

"R-R-Red pill," he said. Then he turned to me. "Bo isn't right. Stay away from him."

I stammered, not knowing what to say.

"His body is dead," Ant'ny said, his eyes staring ahead. "And there's a spirit moving in him."

He grabbed me by my jacket collar. "Why are you surrounded with so much darkness, man?"

"What do you mean?" I asked.

"Whatever's around you, it's dark," Ant'ny said. "I thought I knew you."

He startled at something in the air.

"Do you see that?" he asked, pointing at the sky.

There was nothing there.

A gust blew through the backyard, sending up a column of leaves, carrying a sinister laugh into the night. As it faded, I recognized it as Natkaal.

CHAPTER FIFTEEN

Ant'ny dug his palms into his forehead, grimacing and yelling.

"I can't turn it off," he said, tears in his eyes. "I can't stop seeing."

I laid him down.

"It's going to be all right," I said. "Close your eyes and take a deep breath. I'm not going to let anything happen to you."

I crossed his hands over his chest as he closed his eyes, pressed on them as he breathed in and out in a ragged cadence. He relaxed somewhat, but he wouldn't stop shaking. Moonlight slanted across his face, casting his skin in a navy hue.

Inside, I was freaking out. I had never seen anything like this before in all my years practicing the dark arts. Worst of all, whatever curse Ant'ny was fighting had probably been meant for *me*. I cursed Natkaal under my breath. I'd pissed that grasshopper demon off something awful—and now *I* was pissed something awful. I wasn't sure which was worse, because now I wouldn't be able to rest until I figured out how to outmaneuver him. It was like he invited me to the greatest game of chess ever, and it was my move.

"Uh, boss man," Bo said, "you called me an idiot."

"Not now, Bo," I said.

"I might be an idiot, but I know a curse when I see it. I think Natkaal opened up Ant'ny's third eye."

I closed my eyes.

"How about you tell me something good for a change," I said.

"Before you put me in this body, I saw everything," Bo said. "Odd energies, auras, a lot of stuff that is unspeakable and has no word in the English language to describe it."

"Don't remind me," I said.

"When you put me in this body, I lost that supernatural sight," Bo said. "But I still sense things on a higher level from time to time."

He shook his head. "Ant'ny can see what I used to see. And if I'm right, it's enough to make a mortal go insane. It's like shooting your brain with high voltage electricity and never turning it off."

Ant'ny jumped and shivered. I reassured him.

"Boss man," Bo said, "if we don't figure out how to shut Ant'ny's third eye, he'll go insane, kill himself, or both."

Harris leaned against the wall. He was as pale as the moon.

"This is my fault," he said. "I did this."

"No," I said. "Natkaal did this. He used you as a carrier for this curse. I should have seen it coming."

"We're having a great night, aren't we?" Harris asked. "I'll call the department and see if there is anyone who has expertise in curses."

"You don't know that off the top of your head?" I asked.

"We don't exactly have a lot of resources in the Paranormal Crimes Division," Harris said. "People wouldn't be pleased to know that their tax dollars support necromancy, vampire tracking, and werewolf suppression services, if you know what I mean. Our division doesn't get much money and we have to make do with what we've got. That includes a resource shortage."

He ducked into the gangway and made a phone call.

Ant'ny was calmer now.

"How are you?" I asked.

"Better," he said, sitting up.

"Still seeing stuff?" Bo asked.

"You got some explaining to do," Ant'ny said, looking me in the eye.

"I'm a necromancer," I said. "I have the unique ability to speak to the dead and control them."

Ant'ny's jaw dropped.

"I didn't want you to know because it's dangerous," I said. "Bo here isn't my wife's cousin from Oklahoma. He's a spirit that I've recruited from the underworld as my servant. I'm a target and I need his protection."

"*That's* why you smell so funny," Ant'ny said.

"I'll take that as a compliment," Bo said. "But yeah, we got the neighborhood fooled pretty good, don't we?"

Ant'ny rubbed his temples. "So what were y'all doin' at the casino?"

"There's a vampire there who's stirring up a lot of trouble," I said. "If I don't stop her, a lot of bad things are going to happen."

"That's why she tried to shoot you?" Ant'ny asked. "Cuz you're trying to stop her?"

"I don't know who tried to shoot me," I said. "That's a question I'd like to know the answer to myself. Listen. I'm going to do everything I can to help you, but you can't leave us."

"I'm not going anywhere," he said. "What happened to me, Lester?"

"Ever heard of your third eye?" I asked.

"Only in movies," he said.

"It's real," I said. "And when it opens, it's like taking every drug in the world at the same time. You're likely going to be sensitive to anything you see. The first thing is not to be afraid."

Ant'ny gulped. "I should've gone home."

Bo clapped. "Genius! If only you had thought that a few minutes ago, dog." He patted Ant'ny on the shoulder. "I sure hope this doesn't affect our relationship. I don't have anybody else I can trust."

"We're good," Ant'ny said. "I think. I don't even know what to think about all of this. Shit."

"Don't think," Bo said. "It'll help. I got your back."

Harris left the gangway, tucking his phone into his pocket.

"Well, Detective?" I asked.

Harris shrugged. "No one in my office has heard of a third eye incident before. First time for everything, I guess. They recommended talking to a psychic."

Bo laughed. "Some kind of supernatural po-lice y'all are."

"They were kidding, right?" I asked.

Harris shook his head.

"You got a lot of learning to do, then," I said. "That's some raggedy advice, Detective."

"Do you have a better idea?" Harris asked.

"I do, but I can't guarantee that we won't end up in deeper problems before we get there," I said.

"Where?" Bo asked.

I rushed up the stairs into my house, into my kitchen. In the cabinet underneath my telephone, I pulled out a phone book. White pages.

"Those things still exist?" Bo asked.

"No old folks' jokes," I said, thumbing through the pages. Hazel trotted out of the hallway to meet me. She sniffed my leg.

With my finger, I traced the last names until I settled on

my target: JOYNER, C. I wrote the address down on a sticky note and put it in my coat pocket.

"I know someone who can help," I said. "If he's home. A supernatural apothecary."

"I'm intrigued," Harris said.

"Ant'ny, can you handle a car ride?" I asked.

"I think so," he said.

I motioned to Bo, and he grabbed a soda from the fridge. He handed it to Ant'ny.

Hazel growled.

"What's up, Hazel?" I asked.

She darted to the back porch. Harris jumped at her deep, throaty bark.

"What now?" I mumbled under my breath as I stalked onto the porch and peeked between the blinds on the door. My alley was lit up with headlights.

Harris joined me at the window.

"Your sedan's in the middle of the alley," I said. "Maybe it's blocking somebody."

I snatched my leash and clipped it on Hazel. Harris, Bo, and Ant'ny followed me through the backyard as Hazel strained to get to the garage.

When I opened the gate into the alley, the headlights nearly blinded me. Harris's sedan blocked the alleyway.

Hazel barked again, and I tugged her leash, bringing her close. A car was stopped a few yards from my garage. On the other end of the garage, another car was also stopped, its headlights bright and white.

The alley was blocked.

My eyes adjusted to the light. I recognized the headlights.

Blue hatchbacks. This time, silhouettes sat inside, watching us. A knot formed in my throat. Was I ever going to get a break?

"Stay back, Ant'ny," Bo said, pushing me and Ant'ny aside. He stood in front of us. Harris joined him.

A car door slammed. I couldn't tell where it came from. Somehow, having Hazel near me made me as comfortable as if I'd had a gun.

Two silhouettes approached us from either side.

Harris drew his gun.

"Stop!" he cried.

The silhouettes stopped.

"Hands up!" he yelled.

The silhouettes didn't obey.

Ant'ny startled and whimpered. I could tell his third eye was ramping up again.

"Goddamn," he said.

"Be cool," I whispered, holding Ant'ny back. "Remember what Bo said. Don't be afraid."

Ant'ny closed his eyes. I patted him in solidarity.

"Let us handle it," I said.

A fence shook, filling the alley with the subtle sound of rustling metal. Harris aimed his gun across the alley at my neighbor's fence.

Then a female voice spoke out of nowhere.

"Supernatural police," she said, softly. "You got spicy on me, Lester."

We turned around to see Fiona sitting on Harris's black sedan. She grinned, exposing her sharp fangs.

"I thought I told you not to meddle in my affairs," she said. "Guess that means I have to keep my promise."

She hopped down off the car and snapped her fingers. More car doors slammed.

"Time to turn you all into avocado toast."

CHAPTER SIXTEEN

In a millisecond, Fiona was flying at me.
Tap tap.
Harris stood nearby, aiming at Fiona. He had trouble tracking her as she bounded onto the roof of the garage, across the alley, and onto a telephone pole.

Something crashed into me, knocking me into my garage door.

Bo. Fiona crashed into the gate next to my garage as the smell of gun smoke entered my nostrils.

She snapped her fingers and pointed at us. Footsteps scudded across the gravel.

Harris fired.
Tap. Tap. Tap.
I suddenly became aware of the leash around my palms tugging me toward the fight. Then the leash slipped away and dragged against the gravel.

Hazel escaped and rushed at a vampire who was running at me. The guy didn't look any older than thirty. She locked her jaws onto his wrist. The vampire screamed—either in pain or at the fact that his expensive sweater was ruined.

I rushed to my feet and followed up with a swift punch

across the vampire's jaw. It was like punching a sack of potatoes.

The vampire recoiled and stumbled backward with one hand on his jaw, Hazel still connected to his arm.

I knew I had a mean hook, but...I didn't think it was that mean. My fist didn't even hurt, which was unusual. Usually, my knuckles burned raw after a punch like that.

"Hazel, off," I said.

Hazel wouldn't let go.

The vampire reached into his pocket, but Ant'ny jumped onto him and punched him in the face.

Hazel let go.

Ant'ny and the vampire struggled, rolling around. Ant'ny landed on his back. He must have seen the vampire for what it was, because he screamed in terror. One of his fits again.

A shadow flew through the air, and a lone boot passed me, followed by thick legs as Bo drop-kicked the vampire in the chest.

"Didn't yo mama ever teach you not to wear Gucci sweaters to a fight?" Bo asked.

The vampire rolled to his feet and scurried away like a creature, arm bleeding.

I pulled Ant'ny up and tried to comfort him.

"You're all right," I said. "You're all right."

"What the hell are these things?" he asked.

I grabbed him and pulled him away from the fight and toward a fence, but vampires hemmed us in on both sides.

"We're dealing with vampires," I said softly. "Don't let their auras scare you."

"They don't have auras," Ant'ny said. "That was what scared me."

"Concentrate on me," I said, grabbing Ant'ny by the shoulders. "Sorry you have to go through this, but we'll get out of it okay."

Bo pointed at the telephone pole where Fiona was watching.

"Man shrimp versus vampire, round two," he said.

Harris backed toward us. Another vampire shambled in our direction. This one was a female in a leather jacket. She had a bullet hole in her shoulder and one of her legs.

Harris aimed at her, but in a flash, Fiona kicked him in the back and clotheslined Bo. Neither saw her coming.

I had just enough warning to see a roundhouse kick aimed at my face.

Instinctively, I grabbed Fiona's ankle. I saw the horrified look on her face as I swung her around and launched her at the wall in my garage. The panels caved like a house of cards, and she smashed into a rack of tools on the back wall. They toppled off the shelf, burying her in a rain of drills and hammers.

"That's what I'm talkin' about, boss man!" Bo said, raising his fists to his face.

What the hell? I knew Fiona was a lightweight, but not even Bo would have been able to do that. My muscles didn't even hurt. The muscles in my arms told me "more, more, more." I had never felt this sensation before, like I wanted to take on all the vampires in the alley and rip them apart—and still, that wouldn't have been enough. I stumbled backward against my body's will.

Bo coughed and struggled to his knees. Ant'ny and I joined him. Harris scrambled for his gun and stood next to us.

Hazel dashed to my side and barked at Fiona.

For a moment, we looked like a real crew. No one was gonna mess with me and my boys tonight.

Fiona jumped to her knees, pure fear and embarrassment on her face for a split second before it flashed away to a growl.

"Come and get you some more of this sweet power, baby," Bo said. He cocked his head to the vampires on both sides of us with a sly grin. They stopped approaching, shock on their faces. "That includes y'all bloodsuckers too."

Fiona was about to respond, when a shrill chirp stopped her.

The bite marks in my wrist burned and I cupped it.

The vampires behind us stared at a telephone pole across the alley. A brown bat rested on one of the foot hooks, chirping at us. If I didn't know any better, I'd say it was grinning at us. It flapped its wings a few times, moonlight exposing the veins in them, and it nodded its head up and down, wrinkling its stubby nose and revealing two protruding fangs.

"You're scum!" Fiona cried.

At first, I thought she was talking to me, but in the sycamore tree behind the pole, dozens of silvery eyes glowed like fireflies.

"You won't stop me," Fiona said, grabbing a drill. She launched it at the bat, but it lifted off just before the drill cracked against the wood.

The sycamore leaves rustled and then, bats were everywhere. The sky was covered with them.

A deluge of shrieks entered the garage and I dragged Bo down. The things were so loud, I couldn't hear. A sea of brown covered everything.

A nagging voice in my head told me to *stay down*. Normally, I wouldn't have listened, but I obeyed. I was happy to get some help, but I knew these damn bats weren't my friends.

A few seconds later, the sea of brown subsided, and the shrieking faded, overtaken by the sound of screeching tires and revving car engines.

Fiona and her vampires were in their hatchbacks. Fiona hung out of the moonroof of one of the cars, surrounded by a faint pink bubble.

"I can play dirty too," she said as a column of bats swirled around her. She glanced at me for a moment and said, "What a pleasant and useful surprise."

She smirked, held out her hands, and chanted something familiar…

Another language. Some kind of tongue that didn't make any sense.

I'd heard that language before. I knew the sharp vowels and consonants that barreled against the back of the mouth…

The language of demons.

A pentagram blossomed around Fiona's head like a halo, and two orange jewel slits for eyes blinked open inside it.

"Run!" I cried, grabbing Ant'ny. Hazel followed.

Bo and Harris stood, staring at Fiona.

I yelled at them again. This time, they heard me.

We ran into my backyard as a pink blast ripped through the alley and through Harris's sedan. The car twirled through the alley like a coin, then crashed and rolled several times before bursting into another explosion that rocked the alley.

I covered my face as a wave of heat blew over me.

The engine revved, bat shrieking, and explosions gave way to a welcome quiet of crackling fire and distant sirens.

I stood, wobbling to my knees. My knees screamed. I didn't do myself any favors by throwing myself down. I already had too much crap to deal with—I didn't need my knees giving up on me either.

"What the heck was that?" Harris asked.

We walked into the alley, and into a wall of smoke.

I stepped on something soft and moist.

A bat. Dead. Its tongue hung out of its mouth.

Dozens of bats lay dead in the alley.

"Those aren't bats, are they?" Ant'ny asked. "They're part of something bigger, something darker. I don't understand what I'm seeing."

"Long story," I said. "I'll catch you up later."

Shadows flapped overhead, and I saw the flock covering the moon as it shrieked ever high into the sky.

Fiona had killed some of them, and they were reeling from the attack. What did that mean symbolically?

Under normal circumstances, I would have tried to thank them, but these weren't normal circumstances.

Had Fiona wounded the Vampire Collective consciousness in some way? This night was getting weirder and weirder. I groaned as I thought about the consequences of an all-out vampire war—with little ol' me on the frontlines. A necromancer holding the fate of the vampire race in his hands... who knew?

"I'm gonna catch hell for this," Harris said, studying what was left of his car. The crumpled sedan was burning like a steak out of control on a grill.

"Good Lord," I said.

Bo scratched his head. "Yo, boss man, I wanna know somethin'."

"Lay it on me," I said.

"How'd you launch that chick into the garage? You been working out and not telling me?"

"Beats me," I said. "But it looks like that vampire bite gave me more than just a curse. I must have gotten some of their super strength."

"Daaaaaaaamn," Bo said. "And second thing, why does Fiona have a demon hanging around her?"

"That's what I want to know," Harris said.

"She told me she did shadow deals," I said, "but I didn't know she was that cozy with a demon. I've never heard of a vampire working with a demon before. It's...unorthodox."

I remembered the demon's opal eyes.

This was, by far, the craziest night of my life and I still had no idea what was going on or how to fight back. Ant'ny's third eye was opened against his will, I had vampire powers all of a sudden, and I was up against a foe who was ten thousand steps ahead of me.

There was only one person who might be able to help me. And, boy, was he going to be pissed at me for visiting him unannounced at this time of night. If I could find him.

The police sirens were closer now.

Harris sighed.

I motioned to Bo. "Take Ant'ny and Hazel, get the car, and wait for me up front."

Bo saluted and jumped into the car. Ant'ny followed with Hazel, and Bo gunned it out of the alley.

Harris stood, hands in his pockets, surveying the carnage.

"Jesus," he said. "When I joined the Supernatural Crimes Division, I thought I knew what I was getting into."

"Looks like you got a lot of explaining to do to your colleagues, Detective," I said, grinning. "You won't mind if we scoot out of here, do you?"

"You have my cell," Harris said. "What's your next step?"

"I need to pay an associate a visit," I said. "I need to stop Fiona, but I've got to look out for Ant'ny. He's in trouble."

The sirens were a block away now.

"Mr. Broussard," Harris said sternly as primary lights washed across the alley, "I hope this isn't the last time I see you."

"If it is, it won't be intentional," I said, waving as I retreated into the shadows of my backyard.

CHAPTER SEVENTEEN

"You sure we got the right address?" Bo asked as we eased down a residential boulevard with three-story brick rowhouses.

I unfolded a piece of paper from my coat pocket and read it again. Before I jumped in the car, I had pulled Cassius Joyner's home address from the white page phonebook in my hallway.

Don't judge—yes, I use a phonebook. And yes, I'm old-school. Joyner was from the older school—probably impossible to find him using an internet search. Supernatural apothecaries don't like to draw attention to themselves.

We were a few neighborhoods away in the Soulard neighborhood. Joyner ran an apothecary in Soulard Market, and he lived only a few blocks from the market.

Bo stayed in the center of a narrow street surrounded by brick row houses on both sides.

St. Louis is a city of neighborhoods. Each one has its unique flavor. Soulard is like a glimpse into the city's past, with a touch of France. The houses here were skinny and narrow, with long, stately rectangular windows, ornate shutters, and shingled roofs with striking, decorated dormer windows. On some of the streets, you got a pop of color as the houses changed from red to purple to yellow. They don't make houses like that anymore.

Every now and again, Bo had to stop and let a car pass since the streets were so narrow.

During the day, you could smell fried meat from Soulard Market, one of the largest indoor farmers' markets in the country. And you could hear musicians playing songs—a jazz guitar or a lone sax playing the blues. But at night, it was quiet around here. When the market closed and all the foot and car traffic slowed down, it was like any other STL neighborhood —never-ending and dark. For all the taxes we paid, you'd expect the city to be lit up like a Christmas tree at night. The least they could do was install a few extra streetlights. That's my tax dollars at work.

"Can't see the house numbers," Bo said, straining over the steering wheel. "Ant Man, why don't you put that third eye to work and help a brother out?"

"Doesn't work that way," Ant'ny said. He hadn't said anything the entire car ride and had a sullen, sober look on his face, staring ahead and at nothing at all. Hazel was resting, her head on his lap. He stroked her back.

"Joyner lives at 23 and a half," I said, scanning the houses on my side. "My side's got even numbers, so keep looking."

Bo groaned. "These damn house numbers, man."

The car halted quickly. I flew forward, slammed into my seat, and looked at him angrily.

"Hehe," he said. "Found it."

The house in question was a brick house with a freshly painted black door set into an alcove, which made it hard to see from the street. A lone lamp in the alcove was unlit. The address was lacquered on the door in gold letters. One of the numbers hung loose. Windowsill planters presented bright yellow flowers, and they dripped water from a recent evening watering session. The curtains on all three levels of the house were drawn.

"Uh, boss man, you sure this is it?" Bo asked.

Either Joyner was going to be surprised to see me, pissed off, or both. If he was home.

Bo parallel parked between two sedans and glanced at the door again.

"Sure hope apothecary man is home," he said. "You think he might be able to re-up some of my stash?"

The last time we visited Joyner, he gave Bo a bottle of mint, myrrh, and a blend of essential oils that helped mask his usual stench of Polo cologne and rotting flesh. Boy, was I grateful for that. If you ever meet Bo sometime, you'll thank Joyner for saving your nostril hairs, because my buddy can get funky.

"Ant'ny, we're going to visit a friend of mine," I said. "He's a supernatural apothecary."

"A supernatural what?" Ant'ny asked.

"He's like a pharmacist, but for people like me and Bo," I said.

"Y'all are into some crazy shit," Ant'ny said.

"You're not lying," I said, "but Joyner can probably whip up a concoction that might help you with the third eye problem."

"While you're at it," Bo said, scratching his head, "Tell him I got this foot fungus that I'm trying to solve. It's green and crusty, and—"

I swatted Bo away. Ant'ny let out a "good lawd" and turned away in disgust. Bo grinned and wagged a finger at us.

"Just kiddin'," he said.

We all got out of the car and stood on the sidewalk in front of Joyner's house, staring up at it. A truck passed on the street behind us.

"Ant'ny and I will go in," I said. "Bo, you and Hazel are on security duty."

"You hear that, Hazel?" Bo asked, tipping his sunglasses at her. "That means any fools that come through here trying to start trouble are liable to get punched or bitten. We're gonna be a dynamic duo, I just know it."

Hazel tilted her head at him. I told her to stay, and she yawned and sat in the front of the alcove next to Bo. Bo stood like a sentinel with his arms crossed. For what it was worth, his tracksuit was giving off an extra "don't fuck with me" vibe tonight, and lord knows I needed that.

The door was black with an all-glass panel and a mosaicked transom at the top. I rapped on the door and waited, staring through the glass panel. Somewhere, another siren sounded.

I just needed Joyner to be home. I didn't deserve much in life, but I needed a lucky break every now and again. I was going to owe Joyner big time if he helped me out, and I thought of how many tallies to the bad I'd be after this.

After a minute, I knocked again and waited, hardly able to exhale.

Suddenly, the curtain on the other side of the glass panel parted. An old black man with liver spots on his bald head stared at me angrily.

"Mr. Joyner, it's me," I said.

The curtain fell back into place. A few seconds later, the deadbolt unlocked and the door flew open. The short, bald man stood on the threshold wearing a white tank top, khaki shorts, and brown dress socks hiked up to his knees. He leaned on a cane.

"My shop is closed after five," he said with a gravelly voice. "And I don't do after-hours visits."

"I'll pay you after-hours fees if you want," I said. "But I'm in a world of trouble and need help."

Joyner grinned, revealing a big gap between his two front teeth.

"You said that last time," he said. "I assume the chakra tea I gave you musta turned out okay."

During my last adventure, Joyner brewed a tea that helped me open up my chakras so that I could sense a gang of angry jinn who wanted to do me harm. When all my chakras opened, I became hyper-aware of everything around me. I could only imagine what Ant'ny was seeing.

I stared at Joyner, and he stared back at me for a few seconds. Then he looked at Ant'ny.

"Ah, I see why you're here now," he said. "Young man, you got a third eye in your forehead that's as big as a baseball. You know that?"

Ant'ny scratched his shirt collar. "It sucks, man."

Joyner puffed. "Sucks is an understatement. Maybe one of these nights I'll be able to have some proper quiet time."

He retreated into the darkness of his house and waved us in.

Ant'ny and I looked at each other and then followed Joyner into his home and shut the door.

A sole television played in the living room off to the left, giving off an ethereal glow in the dark house. On the television, a preacher in a double-breasted pinstripe suit strode around on a church stage, waving his hands wildly and shouting about how folks ought to wake up because they were sleeping on the Lord.

"I'm not a gambling man," Joyner said as we followed him into his kitchen, "but you had something to do with that breaking news explosion I saw on the news."

Joyner had that old-school, sing-songy rhythm to his voice. Always reminded me of my grandpop. He talked *fast*, like his mind was generating words faster than he could say them.

"If you were a gambling man, you would have won," I said.

Joyner's kitchen was tiny. A gas stove, an old white refrigerator, and a rickety metal table with 50s-style diner chairs. He gestured for us to sit. Even though the neighborhood had gentrified, Joyner's house looked like it hadn't aged since he bought it. The cabinets and linoleum floors harkened back to an older time. I suppose a supernatural apothecary had bigger things to worry about.

Joyner flicked the light on, filling the kitchen with fluorescent blue.

"So what's happening, Mr. Broussard?" he asked, concerned.

I told him everything, and his eyes widened. Then he frowned as if he had eaten a bad meal. The story visibly disturbed him.

"Sometimes when customers come to see me at the shop," he said, "they have little problems. How come every time I see you lately, the world is at risk?"

"That's the game of necromancy, I guess," I said. "My focus is Ant'ny. Can you help him with this third eye?"

Joyner scrutinized Ant'ny. The old man's gaze made him uncomfortable and he looked away.

"No, don't look away," Joyner said. "I need to get a good look at you."

Ant'ny looked back at Joyner as the old man approached him, leaning on his cane.

"Ah-ha," Joyner said. "I understand now. Well, Mr. Broussard, do you want the bad news or the god-awful news first?"

"No good news?" Ant'ny asked.

"The demon's curse isn't permanent," Joyner said. "Not unless you want it to be. But that isn't what you want to hear, young man."

"Give us the worst of it," I said. "After all I've been through tonight, I can handle it."

Joyner opened a cupboard. I expected to see cups. Instead, there were terrariums—some shaped like curved fish bowls, others like aquariums, and others like bird cages—and they were overflowing with herbs. He picked a few of them into his palm. He swung out a lazy Susan and collected a couple of bottles of essential oils and dried slivers of skin that looked like kiwis—but whatever they were, they weren't kiwis.

"The bad news is that even though the curse isn't permanent, it can kill you," Joyner said. "It'll break your mind if you're not careful. You're completely at the whims of whatever supernatural creature you come across. Your third eye is liable to be your biggest liability. So you might want to stay home. But I also suspect that staying home probably isn't safe now, is it?"

"He stays with me," I said. "I'm responsible for this."

"That was what I feared," Joyner said, setting a mortar and pestle on the table. "I can give you something that will relax you and make you a little less sensitive so your eye won't open up all the time. If you want to eliminate the condition, though, you got to go back to the source."

"You mean the thing that did this to me?" Ant'ny asked.

"That leads me to the god-awful news," Joyner said, grinding the herbs. "You can make a deal with the demon who cast the curse, or you can kill it. Both will cure your condition. Both come with undesirable consequences, though, but I don't need to tell you that, Mr. Broussard."

I cursed.

Natkaal had me right where he wanted me—by the balls. The demon had helped me in my last adventure. Funny how the tide turned. He was going to make good on his promise to keep me locked out of necromancy unless I went to him first.

"So what do we do, Lester?" Ant'ny asked. "Sounds like I'm all kind of f—"

I waved a hand. It wasn't good form to curse in front of Joyner. Old-school black folks around here didn't like profanity. They're salt of the earth, right versus wrong kinda folk. Once, my neighbor Granny gave me hell for saying the word hell. I can barely say hash brown heck around her without getting smacked with a newspaper.

Joyner didn't hear the comment. The old man whistled as he whipped up a concoction in his mortar. He ground the herbs down to a nice paste, sprinkled some oregano in it, then filled it with water and poured the water into a plastic medicinal pouch. He put the pouch in the microwave for a minute and slid out a black bandanna from another drawer. The microwave dinged, and he wrapped the pouch in the bandanna and handed it to Ant'ny.

"Whoo wee, you put me to work tonight," Joyner said, wiping his brow. "Haven't done a spell like that in a long time."

"What's in here?" Ant'ny asked incredulously, holding the pouch.

"Little bit of holy basil in there to give it a good smell," Joyner said, tapping the pouch with his index finger. "But it's an old-school mix of lavender, ashwagandha, raccoon skin, and lemon balm, among other things."

"Raccoon skin?" Ant'ny asked.

I laughed. "Let me guess—trickster DNA, eh?"

"That's right," Joyner said. "It's meant to calm your mind and distract your third eye. The coon skin will do that. It will soothe some of the irritation around your third eye. It works best a few minutes after you've heated it up."

"I appreciate it, Mr. Joyner," I said, slipping him a fifty.

"Any time," Joyner said. He pocketed the cash but didn't move. He stared at me, thinking.

Here we went again. Sometimes, you couldn't just buy stuff from another supernatural. Sometimes, you also had to do them favors.

"There's something else you can do for me since you're here," Joyner said. "If you don't mind?"

I couldn't exactly say no. After all, I was the one who came to him after hours.

I put my hands in the pockets of my gabardine and spread the coat back. "What's up, Mr. Joyner?"

He motioned for me to follow him.

Joyner led us down a door and into an uncomfortably narrow stairwell. The smell of the old basement hit me hard. A lot of old basements in the city smelled dreadful. Finished basements weren't a thing around here.

I expected to walk into a concrete wonderland, maybe with some metal beams, a sad furnace, and an egress window or two. What I got was a botanical wonderland.

There were herbs in pots everywhere, ranged in rows. Long grow lights in the ceiling lit up the place in a neon pink that reminded me of the red light district in Amsterdam. The walls had a texture that looked like a hybrid between metal and frosted glass, and they mirrored our blurry reflections as we passed. The air was water-kissed and so intensely floral that it was sickening.

"Damn," Ant'ny said under his breath. "This place is off the hook."

"Young man, they don't make hooks big enough for greenhouses like mine," Joyner said.

The old man hobbled on his cane through the lanes of plants, and Ant'ny and I followed, spellbound.

I should have been surprised, but I wasn't. Mr. Joyner *had* to have an herb farm to do what he does. It wasn't like he could import his ingredients.

"This is quite a farm you got down here," I said.

"You wouldn't believe how many people I had to talk to to keep it," Joyner said. "First, the utilities turned me in because they thought I was growing the good herb, if you know what I mean. The police and DEA official came 'round and, boy oh boy, they got a kick out of this place."

"I bet they did," I said. "Did you send them home with bouquets?"

Joyner puffed and gave a knowing laugh. "I got left alone for a long, long time. Until now. Some Humpty Dumpty city official is trying to shut me down. Says that neighbors complain about the pink lights. Ain't nobody ever said anything as long as I've lived here."

We stopped at a table of potted flowers. They looked orange, but the pink lights were fooling my eyes. I'm terrible with recognizing plants anyway.

"They're trying to find an ordinance so they can throw the book at me," Joyner said, brushing one of the flowers with a knuckle. "I came home one day and they shut my water off. I paid the bill on time. These fools put me on hold for an hour, only to come on and say it was a technical issue and they were looking into it. Nobody else around here lost water. They restored it, but that was the warning shot. Two days later, I lost an entire row of plants."

He gestured to the long row of flowers. On second inspection, they weren't as vibrant as the others. Some of them were wilting.

"I've only got a few working years left," Joyner said. "Then I'm going on Social Security like everybody else."

The thought of not being able to call Joyner anymore made me sad.

The old man turned to me. "I can't lose this place. It's my only treasure at my age. Lost my wife a few years ago, and I don't see my grandkids much. These flowers are my children."

"I hear you," I said. "But what do you want me to do?"

"Anything you can do to keep me off the city's radar would be appreciated," Joyner said.

I looked around the greenhouse again. The things you see in my city.

As I've said before, necromancy is a game of tallies. You ask the supernatural powers that be for certain favors to advance your agenda.

Every act of necromancy is a tally against you on the celestial scoreboard. Even though I use it for good, that doesn't change its power, and its power to corrupt the fabric of the world. You're changing fate, after all. Necromancy invites bad karma, and you always end up owing someone or *something*. You've got to be a skilled politician and have a good memory about what your tallies are, because if you slip up—well, a demon will end up killing your family and sending your life into abject misery for seven years until you wake up one day and decide you're back in the game. So the game of tallies continues indefinitely until one day you end up in the spirit world. The game is forever.

"I'll see what I can do, Mr. Joyner," I said, extending a hand.

"You're an upstanding gentleman," Joyner said. "It's always a pleasure, Mr. Broussard."

"What are these things?" Ant'ny asked.

He pointed to a cluster of Venus flytraps. Their fleshy mouths were extra pink in the grow lights, and their green stalks were so green, they were almost radioactive. Their mouths were open, teeth fanned out like little knives. They were wilted and didn't look good, like they hadn't been watered in days.

"Those are my Venus flytraps," Joyner said. "Another casualty in my battle with the city."

He lifted one of them from the bottom. It hung limp.

"Not even their fault," Joyner said. "They're endangered, you know. I felt so bad when they died on me. I'm hoping I can save a few."

I crouched to get a better look at the traps. The things were freaky. I never thought carnivorous and plant went in the same sentence, but hey, Mother Nature works in mysterious ways.

I shook my head. "Mmm mmm," I said.

Then I got an idea.

"Mr. Joyner," I said. "What do these things eat?"

Joyner reached under one of the tables and produced a bag of dead crickets.

"Used to feed 'em flies, but I'm not keen on them," he said.

"What else do they eat?" I asked.

"Spiders, wasps—any kind of insect, really," Joyner said.

I grinned.

"How about grasshoppers?" I asked.

CHAPTER EIGHTEEN

"I said it before, and I'll say it again: you crazy," Bo said as we entered my house through the front door.

"I'm not that crazy," I said.

The alley was still cordoned off by police cars, and sirens were awash behind the house. Folks were sitting on their porches, gathered in the street, waiting for some more action. We had to sit in the car, surveying the street for a few moments before slipping out. On nights like this when I was in the middle of a conflict, I didn't exactly like parking in the front of the house and advertising my location, but I didn't have a choice.

At my kitchen table, I emptied the contents of a bag I brought from Joyner's: a bag of peat moss and bottles for Bo's odors. We also stopped at a pet shop on the way home and bought half a dozen live crickets. The crickets crawled in a plastic puff bag between a maze of egg carton scraps that the pet shop employee loaded in before sealing the bag.

Bo lugged in a heavy flower pot of dead Venus flytraps and set it gingerly on the table. Some of the brown and white peat in the flower pot spilled out.

"You're gonna make that demon hella angry," Bo said. He screwed up his face and looked at the plant.

"That's the point," I said.

I took out one of the crickets and walked out to my back porch door. My spider sat on a little web in the eave, staring at me. I stuck the cricket in its web.

"I appreciate your help tonight," I said. "You did me a good job, as always."

I stood on the steps holding my bag of crickets and took in the humid night air. Hazel joined me on the step and I gave her a long pet.

"What a night, huh, sweet pea?" I asked.

Dogs didn't talk back, but they listened. They always had a keen sense of how you were feeling. I always found that it works best to talk to them just like you'd talk to anyone else. Tonight, Hazel wasn't in much of a listening mood. She yawned in response to my question.

There were still a lot of squad cars in the alley. Too many for my liking. Harris was still among the officers. He stood next to a dumpster, his arms were folded as he talked to what looked like a police captain.

I shook my head. Hell of a job he had to explain why a vampire summoned a demon and blew up his assigned car. Nope, the police force wasn't for me.

I took a few minutes circling the house, feeding the crickets to my spiders, thanking them for an all-around good job.

The dead can't technically eat. Bo never gets hungry, and my wallet is thankful for that. But even though The Cluster couldn't technically eat the crickets, they could absorb the moisture from them, which kept them vibrant for me. Plus, the act of consumption kept their spider predatory instincts intact, which was what I needed them for. I see it as a sign of respect to these creatures to give them a life that was as similar as possible to the one they left behind. I've heard stories of necromancers who reanimated corpses and ran them ragged, only to discard them when finished. These necromancers don't realize that necromancy carries with it an immense responsibility to respect the dead. I guess that's why I'm so rare.

When I returned to the kitchen, Bo was helping Ant'ny tie his new black bandanna from Joyner.

"You better get out of here with these weak-ass bandanna ties, Ant Man," Bo said. "If you gonna wear a bandanna around me, you got to look hard."

Bo stepped back, admiring his handiwork. Ant'ny's bandanna had a knot tied in the front, with two floppy strands hanging from his forehead. Reminded me of the way Tupac used to wear his bandannas.

"There we go," Bo said. "Certified gangsta."

"I'll be a gangsta when this is over," Ant'ny said. "Right now, I feel like shark bait."

"Come on now, bruh," Bo said, tapping Ant'ny's chest with the back of his hand. "You gotta be tough. We're gonna get through this together, understand? We got your back."

Ant'ny sighed. "Yeah."

I felt sorry for Ant'ny. There was nothing we could say to shake him from the depression gripping him now. He didn't sign up for this. I'd have to do a lot to make this all up to him once this adventure was over. Our friendship might have been irreparably damaged. He wouldn't be the first friend the dark arts took away from me. The arts have a habit of ruining everything.

"It's all right, Ant'ny," I said. "I'm frustrated too. Maybe we'll be a little less frustrated in a few minutes."

Ant'ny stared at the wall as he talked, disbelief in his eyes. "I can't believe y'all have been doing this stuff right next door."

"Life works in mysterious ways," I said. "The supernatural is best hidden behind closed doors."

"Tell me about it," Ant'ny said, adjusting his bandanna.

"Ant'ny, do you think we can test out Joyner's bandanna?" I asked. "I might need your help downstairs."

"Help with what?" Ant'ny asked.

"Help for the big act," Bo said, grinning. "That thang you saw us doing in the basement."

I grimaced. Those words did not come out right. "Bo, maybe think about how you say that next time."

I opened the kitchen door, told Hazel to stay.

Bo and Ant'ny followed me. My basement was undisturbed since we ran outside and left it in disarray. Several boxes lay on the floor from where Natkaal threw Harris out of the spirit world. Large clods of dirt covered the floor where the magic circle had been.

"What the hell were y'all doing down here?" Ant'ny asked as he crouched underneath the low stairwell.

"Talking to a demon," I said. I clapped a hand on his shoulder. "We're about to speak to it again. Can you handle it?"

Ant'ny's eyes widened. "Speak to a d—"

"It's not for the faint of heart," I said, "and it could trigger your third eye. If it does, maybe you can help."

Bo brushed past me holding the flower pot with the dead Venus flytraps.

"I still think you're crazy," Bo said, sitting the plant down in front of the blanket.

"Crazy is what it's going to take to get us out of this," I said.

Two minutes later, Bo and I cobbled a quick magic circle together: one inner circle with a pentagram, one outer circle, and a blanket and bowl of salt surrounded by flickering candles.

Bo and I sat down on the blanket. Bo placed the flower pot into the inner circle. I motioned for Ant'ny to join us and he squeezed between me and Bo.

"Just stay quiet, Ant'ny," I said. "Let me do all the talking."

Necromancy is about the power of suggestion. I simply suggest that the dead return to life, that's all. This cluster of flytraps was freshly dead; its soul was still warm, which meant I could call it.

Every living thing on this earth leaves behind it a trace of suffering. We're all attached to this big, beautiful planet, and nobody knows when they have an appointment with the reaper.

The natural world is full of attachment; insects crushed under a shoe unexpectedly, or a flower cut off at the stalk by a child wandering through a field one day. Even if a natural thing dies from the law of nature, every living thing has potential, though not all of them achieve it. That creates suffering, and attachment. If you're still attached, I can call you back. Insects, humans, or otherwise—necromancy is necromancy.

These flytraps were just minding their business, taking in light, water, and a healthy diet of crickets from Joyner. Then, one day, the water stopped. I can't imagine the plant's suffering on its way to death.

Until now, I had never called a plant back to life before, but the process was the same.

I focused my concentration on the plant and its dead heads, and I simply suggested that it return to this world. I waved my hand over the stalks and repeated the suggestion—calmly, quietly, like I heard a gardener do once when he was talking to plants.

One of the dead heads lifted and faced my direction.

Ant'ny gasped.

"First time's always freaky," Bo whispered. "Second time is blah."

The head dropped into the peat as if something sliced its life force.

"You may want to close your eyes for a moment," I said.

Ant'ny closed his eyes just as a flash of silver light ripped through the basement. A whipping wind blew hard against my face and it snuffed out my candles. The single light bulb in the ceiling buzzed and sparked out.

We sat in silence for a few moments. A dark shape stood in front of us, just outside the circle.

"You're at it again, Lester," the shadow said. "We never know what to expect from you."

A broad-chested man in a perfectly tailored pinstripe black suit and a red tie spun into an Eldredge knot grinned from next to my washing machine. He wore gaudy golden rings that sparkled in the darkness. His skin was pale, liver-spotted, and utterly and unmistakably cadaverous.

"Mr. Atwood," I said, laughing.

"I had to come see this for myself," Cornelius Atwood said.

"It's not every day I get the big reaper man himself," I said. "How you been?"

Cornelius Atwood was the director of the St. Louis Grim Reaper Society. If you chuckled at the name, I did when I first heard it too. Turns out grim reapers are an organized bunch. People die every minute and the reapers have to be there to ensure their spirits cross from this world to the next. That requires supernatural organizational skills and a leader with a Type A personality. Trust me when I say you don't want to piss Atwood off.

Believe it or not, Atwood made me a grim reaper for a day after my friend Kate was killed so I could investigate her murder. I'll tell you about it sometime.

"You know the protocol," Atwood said, producing a shiny golden coin from his breast pocket. He twirled it between his fingers and it morphed into an hourglass. The sand fell swiftly. "Two minutes to explain to me why you need this Venus flytrap."

If I didn't make my case in two minutes, Atwood would

kill me and take my soul to the great beyond along with the plant. No pressure. As I said, reapers didn't have much time for BS. There was always another soul to collect, and reapers have zero tolerance for fugitive souls. Even being a few seconds late to a death could spell disaster for the reapers, so they ran their schedules like despots.

I told Atwood the abbreviated story of everything that happened so far.

"I only need the plant for tonight," I said. "I'll release it promptly when I'm done."

"I've been doing this for a long time," Atwood said, "but I've never seen this before. What will you give us in return?"

"Same as always," I said. "A favor that is commensurate to the life force of this plant."

"No offense, but that's not much," Atwood said.

"We helped you out before," Bo said. "You know you can rely on us if you need anything."

"That's part of the problem," Atwood said, "Drama follows you."

I shrugged and glanced at the hourglass. Time was running out.

"Very well," Atwood said. "Enjoy your new plant, Mr. Broussard."

The candles lit themselves up and the light bulb flickered on, and Atwood was gone.

I sighed. Looked like I was going to owe a reaper a favor again. But...there were worse people to owe, that was for sure.

"Bo, gather up the dirt on the floor and place it into the flower pot," I said.

Bo obeyed.

You see, when Harris jumped into the spirit world, Natkaal made a mistake. The demon kicked him out and released tons of dirt from the other side. Things over there grow a lot faster and a lot bigger. In my last adventure, CeCe threw diatomaceous earth on my demon adversary and it worked ten times as fast there. The same would be true for dirt brought into this world. Natkaal was in for a thrill.

The heads on the Venus flytrap lifted and oriented themselves toward me as if I were the sun.

"You're one amazing plant," I said. I had to get it to trust me.

I snapped my fingers at Bo and ordered him to get a cup of water.

I bent in front of the plant, studying its green and brown wilted leaves. Nature never failed to amaze me.

Bo returned with a plastic cup of water he drew from the wash sink next to the washing machine.

Bo aimed the cup for the dirt in the flower pot, but I held up my hand, telling him to stop.

"Not yet," I said. "On my cue."

The three of us sat on the blanket in silence.

I took a deep breath, closed my eyes, and said, "Natkaal, I send out a beacon of light to you to ask for your help. Please stop and offer your assistance."

The furnace switched on and blew fire. A papery laugh carried into the basement, crinkling and sinister. Suddenly, the grasshopper demon was hanging over us, grinding its teeth and rubbing its two human hands together. Its red-jeweled eyes gleamed like burning blood.

"How's the third eye curse working out?" he asked.

Ant'ny jolted backward.

"What the—"

Bo grabbed his arm. "Be cool. We're all right."

"It's too bad the curse didn't hit you, Lester," Natkaal said. "Then you would have understood that I was serious when I made my threat."

"You were true to your word," I said. "And I respect that about you. Because of that, I've had a change of heart."

The grasshopper demon grinned. "Oh?"

"The only way to speak to my wife is through you, right?"

I asked.

"Yes," the demon said, descending from the silver thread that hung from the wall. "Yes! Broker me a shadow deal. What problem do you have that your old demon pal Natkaal can solve? Mmm…"

"I have a big problem that you can solve for me right now," I said.

I snapped my fingers. Bo poured the water into the flower pot.

I beamed thoughts to the plant, told it to grow, grow, grow.

The dirt from the supernatural world kicked in fast. The flytrap grew bigger, rising upward, and the traps opened their jaws. Soon, the traps were as big as a kitchen table.

The demon screamed as the plant grew ever upward.

"Whaaaaaat is that?" he asked.

"It's the problem I have," I said, smiling wide.

I willed the traps to start snapping at Natkaal. The jaws opened and closed, narrowly missing the demon's wings.

Natkaal climbed on his string and hung from the ceiling. I willed the plant to grow ever taller.

"Get that thing away!" the demon cried. "Get it away!"

"You know the rules," I said. "You don't get to leave the circle unless I say so or until there's a transaction. Natkaal, do you have any idea what Hydra has been through? She got starved of water, and she's desperate for a meal."

"You stupid necromancer," Natkaal growled.

"You are always true to your word," I said, frowning. "And I'm true to mine, so listen up."

Hydra snapped at him incessantly and he entrenched himself on the wall, his sawtooth mouth contorted into fright.

"If you ever, *ever* try to stand in the way of me or my family when I'm performing the dark art," I said, "you better ask somebody who the hell I am, Natkaal."

One of Hydra's heads narrowly missed Natkaal's wing. I willed the plant to stop growing.

"And you better tell the rest of your friends that I'm not playing games," I said. "You saw what I did to Visgaroth, and whatever he got, you'll get it twice as bad. Got it?"

Natkaal screamed again as Hydra clapped at him.

The demon stammered.

"F—F—F—"

"I can't hear you," I said, cupping my hand to my ear.

"Fine!" Natkaal cried. "Now get that thing off me!"

"No, it doesn't work that way," I said. "Call my wife. Now."

Natkaal's red eyes hardened at me. I didn't know what the demon was thinking, but boy, were its intentions malicious. This thing wanted to kill me something awful.

"You heard me!" I shouted. "I'm losing my patience, Natkaal."

"You're too nice, boss man," Bo said. "Let me translate for my buddy here. Motherfucker, you better call Amira Broussard or Lester's gonna lose his shit."

"Let's go," I said.

"Check yourself before you wreck yourself, bruh," Bo said quickly after me.

Natkaal growled again. "You disgusting sycophantic servant. When you come to Hell, I'll make sure there's a perfect place for you—"

"I'll bring lawn chairs so we can all bake together," I said. "But in the meantime, will you just shut up and call my wife already?"

Natkaal spread his wings. Golden light shone within the wing's veined core. A gray silhouette appeared as if reflected in broken glass. The golden light shone like twilight, illuminating a shapeless face.

"Les?" a female voice asked.

I softened upon hearing my wife's voice. It was the salve I needed on this crazy night with my infected soul.

My lucky break.

CHAPTER NINETEEN

MARRIAGE IS A FUNNY THING.

Some people marry for money and status. Some people marry the person their parents want them to. Others get married out of a sense of duty or commitment to their community. If you're lucky enough to marry for real love—that unshakable, ever-expanding tenderness that knows no bounds, the kind of love that ages like wine—then you will eventually know what it means to suffer. With the exception of motherly love, nobody knows what real love feels like until it's gone. You wake up one morning and you've got this hole in your heart that you can't fill with anything but pain. It might not happen until your spouse dies at a ripe old age, but it'll always get you in the end. In my case, Amira died when we were both forty. Seven years ago.

I'm not a pessimist. I'm just calling it like it is. Most folks in real love don't realize how good they have it. I loved Amira with every inch of my body and spirit. Never had a wandering eye. I was a family man. Every once in a while, I thought, "life could happen," but I didn't think it would be Stage II ovarian cancer.

I still remember rushing her to the emergency room

because of pains in her back. After a night of no sleep and a litany of tests, the doctor gave us the diagnosis, and it hit me like a battering ram. Multiple times. I tried to be strong for Amira, but the truth is that I sat in the chair next to her bed and cried. I had lost my mom and dad two years before, one right after the other. My son and daughter, Marcus and Marlese, were still in high school with their whole lives ahead of them. I wasn't ready to be a single parent. This wasn't the sort of thing that happened to a perfect family, to two people who loved each other.

Marriage is really just problem-solving in disguise. You marry someone who can help you solve problems. Every day in a marriage is a series of problems to solve. Cancer was no different. Together, we beat the disease the first time. When the doctors declared Am's cancer in remission, I was the happiest version of Lester Broussard you ever saw.

When the cancer returned shortly thereafter—when the same back pains that put her in the hospital came blazing in full force—I knew that it wasn't good.

I refused to lose her again. That was right around the time I found necromancy.

I loved my wife so much, I was willing to talk to demons and dead people to save her. Like I said, to be in true love is to suffer.

The first demon I ever spoke to in a magic circle was Visgaroth, and you already know all about him. He taught me everything I knew about unlocking my inner darkness. In a sick and twisted way, that scorpion demon made me who I am—good and bad. And he helped me save Amira from cancer.

Turns out there's a spell for everything—and I mean everything. But it also turns out there are always consequences. Because I didn't understand how shadow deals worked, I never put a time limit on my service to Visgaroth. He treated me like a servant. I was grateful for what he did for me, but I was also an idiot. Visgaroth made me the most powerful necromancer in St. Louis, and I did a lot of demon dirty work. It's the reason I know so much about the supernaturals around here, and why they know me.

One night, Visgaroth asked me to commit a murder. I refused to do it.

It wasn't the cancer that killed Amira—it was Visgaroth. He waited until I went to the grocery store one morning. He broke into my home, tortured her slowly, and waited for me to return home. He broke her neck as I stood on the threshold of my front door holding a bag of zucchinis.

That was how my suffering started, why I bore the pain and guilt of being a necromancer for seven long years. It might as well have been seven decades.

I never thought I'd have the heart to speak to my wife again. I could have called her spirit any time I wanted. I made a promise to my friend CeCe that I would finally do it.

And you know what the first thing out of her mouth was? She forgave me. I spent all this time hating myself, only to be forgiven in one second. That's true suffering—and true love. I guess you could say that's why I use my powers for good; to put some good karma into the world to repay all the damage I did. Amira deserved nothing less.

As I stared at my wife's faceless soul broken up in the reflection of Natkaal's wings, I realized just how bad my night was going, and how I needed a problem solver in crime.

"Les," Amira said sadly. "You shouldn't have called me."

I knew it was her, but I had to be sure. Amira and I had a safe phrase. Sometimes when you spoke to spirits, you weren't always speaking to a spirit, as Natkaal not so kindly demonstrated. The safe phrase helped me avoid traps. After tonight, we'd have to use a new one.

"What does the rosebud say?" I asked.

"Beauty is in the eye of the beholder," Amira said.

I sighed with relief.

"You're breaking every necromancy rule in the book," Natkaal snarled.

"Give me a few minutes and I'll set a record," I said, eyeing the demon for a second. Then I settled back on my wife. "Baby, I need help."

"That's an understatement," Amira said. "I heard you when you tried to call me. I figured you were in trouble."

"I need a clue, something to help me stop Fiona," I said. "She's unlike any other supernatural I've ever met."

"She studied you," Amira said. "She knows everything about you."

"That's what I'm afraid of," I said. "Is there anything about her you can tell me?"

Amira moved a little, casting new golden reflections across Natkaal's wings. I wished I could have seen her face again. Maybe it would have reassured me to see her brown eyes staring back at me, and her micro braids hanging down to one side. Her skin always glowed, just like her golden core was glowing now.

My eyes wandered to Natkaal again. The demon was staring at Ant'ny. I didn't know what the demon was thinking, but it was thinking something. I didn't like it.

"You probably didn't know that Fiona was a student at Wash U," Amira said.

"Before she took a tooth to the neck," I said. "Doesn't surprise me."

Washington University in St. Louis was affectionately dubbed the Harvard of the Midwest. You had to be smart with a capital S to go there. That explained her intelligence.

"This would have been her senior year," Amira said.

My, oh my. To be that young, intelligent, and hatching a dastardly plan. I still couldn't believe it.

"To use a golf analogy, she's one shot away from the hole and I can't even get my ball off the tee," I said.

Bo scratched his head. "What the hell did you just say, man?"

I forgot to introduce Bo.

"Bo, Amira, Amira, Bo," I said.

"Pleasure to meet you," Bo said with a big, ugly smile.

"Don't let Lester boss you around too much," Amira said. "He ought to know how to do his own laundry by now."

I chuckled. I was guilty of off-loading a chore or two. If you had an undead servant with nothing better to do, you'd put him to work too.

"Thank you Jesus," Bo said. "Boss man, I ain't never washin' your draws again."

"I like you already," Amira said. "Les, Fiona was a marketing and economics double major, with honors. She had a steady boyfriend too."

"Boyfriend?" I asked. "She struck me as the forever single type."

"Maybe you should talk to him," Amira said. She gave me a name and an apartment building and number. Her faceless silhouette glanced at Ant'ny.

"Ant'ny, I never thought I'd see you in a magic circle," she said. "I'm sorry for what my husband did to you. I hope you'll forgive him."

Ant'ny was flabbergasted and his mouth hung open. "Lester, you're telling me that…this spirit is Amira?"

"It's her," I said. "You can talk to her directly, you know."

"Be careful with that third eye," Amira said. "Natkaal's curse skills were hot tonight."

"Yes," Natkaal said. A grin spread across his sawtooth mouth and I knew something was coming. "Suppose you gave me the satisfaction of opening it up for just a few moments so I could see my handiwork…"

"Natkaal, I told you I wasn't playing games," I said. "Shut up."

The flytraps sprang to life again and snapped under his wings.

"Don't listen to grasshopper man," Bo said.

"But he should know the horrors of the night that await him," the demon said.

"Natkaal!" I said, raising my voice.

Upstairs, the phone rang. Hazel barked and whimpered.

"Come on, human," Natkaal whispered. "Do it for me just once."

Hazel barked again, this time in rhythm with the phone.

"Amira, there's one more thing I want to ask you about," I said, trying to concentrate.

"Come on, human!" Natkaal asked.

Hazel started scratching the door as the phone rang again. I lost my concentration.

One of Hydra's heads clamped shut. The demon cried out in pain as a trap's teeth ensnared one of his grasshopper legs. He screamed and beat at the flytrap, but the head wouldn't open.

"You will pay for this, necromancer!" Natkaal said.

Damn it. If Natkaal wasn't going to kill me now, I was guaranteeing his wrath.

"Am, when the Vampire Collective bit me, they infected my blood and my soul," I said quickly. "How do I—"

Hazel growled and barked again, louder this time. The damned phone kept going and going.

"Les, it's complicated," Amira said. "You should—"

Natkaal roared and stared at Ant'ny again, emitting circles of light from his eyes that beamed directly into Ant'ny's forehead.

"Open it up, you fool!" the demon said.

Reflexively, I willed the flytrap to rip and tear. Natkaal's leg flew off in a ragged motion. Blue blood spilled across the floor, splattering on me, Bo, and Ant'ny.

Ant'ny screamed.

"No," he said. "No, no!"

Bo grabbed him. "Stay still, man."

Natkaal stared at his leg in horror, unable to comprehend what had happened. Then he screamed too, a banshee-like shriek ripping through the basement.

My egress windows shattered. The light bulb cracked and the filament buzzed, caught fire, and fizzled out.

"Baby," I said.

The phone rang again.

Hazel barked and scratched at the door and pounded at it with her nose.

Ant'ny crawled forward.

"Ant'ny, stop!" Bo cried.

"Baby!" I said.

"Les," Amira said, her voice frightened. "I told you, you have to—"

Amira's soul shimmered inside of Natkaal's wings and disappeared in a flash of light.

Ant'ny clutched his forehead. Blue demon blood glowed on his bandanna. He brought his hands up before his eyes and said, "Aww, hell naw!"

"It's cool, it's cool, it's cool," Bo said fast, grabbing his arm. "Just be patient—"

"I can't do this," Ant'ny said. "I won't let him get to me!"

He stumbled up, accidentally kicking the flower pot over. Peat spilled out all over the inner circle. Hydra's heads crashed to the floor, reared up a final time, and then fell lifeless into the peat. I had lost my link with it and it was forever gone.

Shoe scuffs drew my attention to Ant'ny, who was on his knees now.

"Ant'ny, don't leave the circle!" I cried.

But it was too late. His shoes scuffed the chalk of the outer circle, breaking the clean line that I had drawn.

An explosion tore through the basement. The next thing I knew, I was sliding down the wall.

Two hands grabbed me by the collar and my basement spun around until intense heat licked the back of my shirt.

My furnace. Something kicked the grate off and jammed my head over the lip of the door.

Two gigantic jeweled eyes stared at me, and a putrid mouth of saw teeth that smelled like feces and mold took my breath away.

Natkaal. He had escaped the magic circle.

"Maybe *you* ought to ask somebody before you screw around with a demon," Natkaal said.

Flames singed my hair just as a piece of wood splintered and flew in every direction.

The demon let me go and whipped around.

Ant'ny held a splintered two-by-four. From the horrified look on his face, his third eye was open.

"Fine," Natkaal said. "You die first!"

Natkaal lunged at Ant'ny, but he stepped aside. The demon slashed its wings, but Ant'ny seemed to predict what it was going to do and ducked just at the right moment.

Natkaal snapped its jaws at Ant'ny, backing him up against the wall.

I rolled away from the furnace, panting.

Bo lay against the wall, chin slumped against his chest. Little chirping birds might as well have been circling his head.

I had an idea.

I dashed up my stairwell. Hazel's barking grew louder.

I opened the door. Hazel growled and dashed downstairs and past me. She stopped at the base of the stairs and barked at the demon.

Natkaal ignored her; he was still swiping at Ant'ny and missing every shot. Ant'ny ducked under a wing slash and rolled under the demon, avoiding a hard stomp. Then the demon turned and grinned evilly at Hazel.

The demon limped toward Hazel, blue blood dripping from its severed leg.

I crouched and snuck around the other side of the furnace and found the same stack of two-by-fours that Ant'ny had found.

I swiped a piece of lumber and stuck it in the furnace flames. The end caught fire like a torch.

Natkaal approached Hazel slowly. I approached the demon from behind, aiming for the demon's back.

"No, Lester, his wings!" Ant'ny cried.

I obeyed and swung the burning lumber as hard as I could.

One of Natkaal's pretty little wings shattered.

The demon screamed.

Hazel lunged and latched on to one of its human hands.

"Nooooooo!" Natkaal cried.

Bo startled awake.

"Whoa!" he said, jumping to his feet.

He ran, jumped, and punched Natkaal in one of its eyes.

The demon shrieked and turned into a burning spear as it landed in the spot where one of my egress windows was. Then it squeezed through, screamed into the dark night, and was gone.

Bo, Ant'ny, and I stood, surveying the battle scene: the broken magic circle covered in peat, zigzagging trails of blue demon blood, wood splinters everywhere, and the gossamer membranes of the demon's wings melting into the concrete.

"Did we just release a demon into the city?" Bo asked incredulously.

"Yep," I said, "just like last time."

"And he was mad as hell, wasn't he?" Bo asked, scratching his head.

"Yep," I said. "Just like last time…"

"Fiona Schmiona," Bo said. "Now we got bigger problems."

CHAPTER TWENTY

Harris was the one who had called me when I was talking to Natkaal. None of this was his fault, but I was grumpy when I called him back.

"Mr. Broussard, any luck with a remedy for the third eye?" he asked.

"No," I said. Behind me, Bo brought a dustpan full of peat from the basement and emptied it into the trash can in the kitchen. Ant'ny stood on the porch and stared wistfully out the window. His bandanna was wet from washing Natkaal's demon blood from it. I still had a splotch of dark blue blood on my gabardine. I'd have to throw it away after tonight.

"You'll be glad to know we're in the clear," Harris said. "A tow truck will be moving my burned car shortly. The city is investigating it as an arson."

"That's a relief," I said flatly.

"Well?" Harris asked. "Do *you* have any good news?"

"We got our lead," I said. I repeated the name and the address that Amira had given me.

"Really?" Harris asked, brightening. "Nice work."

"We'll see about that," I said. "We're leaving in five."

Harris told me he'd have someone run a background check on a Mr. Branford Lamar, and that he'd meet us there.

I hung up.

"Basement's all clean," Bo said, wiping his hands. "It's a shame we had to throw Hydra away. I was beginning to like her."

I ignored him.

"Ant'ny," I said.

He ignored *me*.

"Next time I tell you to stay inside a magic circle, listen to me," I said. "I don't feel like getting killed on a technicality."

"You could say thanks for helping you," he said.

I joined him on the porch. Outside, a tow truck beeped its way back into the alley.

I softened a little. I had to get that off my chest. Getting cut off from Amira and not hearing her final answer had ticked me off.

"My eye helped me," Ant'ny said. Suddenly, he grinned. "Did you see me dodging that demon?"

Bo gave a loud guffaw. "You looked like the black version of an out-of-shape Jackie Chan." Bo did a karate chop followed by a kick. He lost his balance and stumbled into the wall.

"Y'all didn't see that," he said. "But yeah, Ant Man, you killed it."

"Joyner's remedy worked," Ant'ny said.

I cracked a smile. "And we're all grateful for it. But follow instructions next time."

I scooped my keys out of my gabardine and waved them. "Let's ride, gentlemen."

～

Wash U is near Forest Park. Bo took side streets to Forest Park Parkway, a long, winding tree-lined road that ran alongside

Forest Park, one of the crown jewels of my city. The street, rimmed with orangish-yellow tungsten street lights, runs parallel to the MetroLink, which is our city's version of a slow-speed public rail system. A train scooted by, carrying what looked like a bunch of St. Louis Cardinals fans dressed in red and white baseball shirts, probably coming from a game downtown. Forest Park was quiet tonight, barely visible over the tall walls that divided it from the MetroLink tracks. Then, suddenly, we were driving alongside an institution that looks like it was transplanted straight out of England.

Many out-of-towners who have never been to St. Louis before are taken aback by Wash U's decidedly Ivy League look when they roll up on the school's campus. The long, imposing apartment building we were currently looking at, with dusky red bricks set off with stone in the buildings' corners, elaborate arches, and ornate reliefs over the windows reminded me of somewhere over the pond. I read in the newspaper once that this type of architecture was supposed to make you feel like you were a part of something bigger than yourself and render you in awe of the institution. Seemed like a successful design to me.

Wash U is also home to a stellar undergraduate university, medical school, and law school. People around here held it in high esteem.

My wallet cries every time I think about tuition at this place. It'll cost you an entire salary to put your kid up here. And that's just if you want them to subsist on ramen noodles and peanut butter sandwiches. My son Marcus applied here. Instant rejection. I'd be shocked if they even reviewed his paperwork. I wanted my son to have the best, but boy, did I dodge a money bullet. He ended up going to St. Louis Community College, which wasn't bad, but it wasn't top tier.

Marcus's friend was the high school valedictorian. He had straight-A's since kindergarten, scored forty kajillion on the SAT, ran quarterback on the varsity football team, and volunteered at his local pet shelter to pad out his application, and WashU didn't take *him*. He ended up going to Stanford instead on a full ride. Oh, the humanity.

Bo turned left into a parking semicircle in front of the apartment buildings. He eased the car into the fire lane. Bo didn't care tonight and neither did I.

"That's it," I said, confirming the name etched in stone on the building.

"You need a keycard to get in," I said, spotting a box with a blinking red light next to the front door.

Bo turned to me, then at Ant'ny. "There's an easy way to solve this. Eenie, meenie, mynie…"

He finished a finger game and settled on Hazel.

"All right, girl," he said. "This is what you gotta do. Go up to the door, wait for the next college student to come out, give them your best beady anime eyes, and then we'll sneak in while they're busy petting you."

Hazel licked her lips and looked out the window, ignoring him.

"You don't want to do it?" Bo asked. "I'm gonna remember how you snubbed me. That means you're up, boss man."

"Why me?" I asked.

"Colleges are tight about security," Bo said. "Might even be a camera or two around here somewhere. If somebody sees you, they'll think you're someone's out-of-touch dad, have sympathy for you, and hold the door open."

"I resent that characterization," I said.

To be fair, I was wearing a button-down shirt, gray slacks, and a long beige gabardine.

"Put your glasses on too," Bo said, grabbing my glasses case from the glove department. "And when they come out, do that thang you do to me when you're trying to make me feel stupid."

"What?" I asked.

Bo put my glasses on, then he looked at me over the tops of the glasses and impersonated me.

"Bo, will you just shut up?" I asked.

Ant'ny laughed. "Maybe you ought to dress up as Lester for Halloween."

I turned around and stared angrily at Ant'ny for a few seconds. Then I swiped my glasses from Bo and said, "If this was any other night, you'd be walking home."

I got out and walked up to the front door, with my glasses on. Through a small window on the door, I peered into a stairwell and another metal door that led down a long, carpeted hallway of apartment entrances. I stood for a few moments peering in the window, then glanced around the campus.

Something caught my eye.

A shiny, green motorcycle rested in one of the numbered parking spots in front of the building.

The same motorcycle I'd seen at the fried chicken joint. The guy riding it had tried to kill me.

My heart pounded. I wanted to run to tell Bo, but to my surprise, I heard footsteps in the stairwell. Two young Indian men in backpacks pushed out the front door.

I smiled and nodded to them, and they held it open for me.

I thanked them, slipped into the stairwell, and waited for the two students to disappear around the corner before motioning to Bo and Ant'ny.

"Bo, look out the window at ten o'clock," I said. "Do you see that motorcycle?"

Bo cursed.

"Yep. It's even got the bullet holes where I shot it," he said.

"You thinking what I'm thinking?" I asked.

"Time to go catch us a fool," Bo said.

"He's in Apartment 3C," I said as we hurried up the stairwell. Luckily, we didn't pass anyone else.

We opened the third floor hallway door and entered the

long hallway of apartments. 3C was right in the middle of the hallway.

Despite the building's English architecture, the inside was modern, with dark carpeting, sconces next to every door, and cork boards every few feet advertising events going on around campus.

We stopped in front of the turquoise door to apartment 3C.

Bo and I communicated with our eyes. I tapped Ant'ny on the shoulder and said, "He won't recognize you. Just get him to open the door and we'll handle the rest."

Ant'ny nodded and took a deep breath. Bo and I each took a side next to the door as he rapped on the door several times.

Silence.

Ant'ny rapped again.

Bo and I looked at each other. I made a confused face to him, and he shrugged.

Then a metallic click sounded on the other side of the door and my heart stopped.

But Ant'ny's third eye must have been working faster than my human sense—he dove down the hallway a half-second before I cried, "Ant'ny, get down!"

Bullets tore through the door.

Blam! Blam! Blam! Blam! Blam!

Then a gun clicked.

The door flew open, and a black man in a checkered racing jacket and a black-visored motorcycle helmet broke out, charging down the hallway. A tangle of twisted locks bounced behind him as he ran.

Bo took off after him.

I pulled Ant'ny up and we followed.

The man sped down the stairwell, taking two steps at a time. Bo gained on him.

Soon, he pushed out the front door and into the night, and we chased him into the parking lot.

Bo, instead of giving chase, ran to the car, opened the passenger side door, and pulled out my pistol.

The man hopped on his motorcycle, revved it, and guided it into the semicircle in front of the apartment.

Bo quickened his run, but the bike zoomed past him.

A shot rang out. The rear wheel of the bike exploded and sent the man smashing to the ground with a hard thud, metallic screeches, and a rash of sparks. He slammed into a red station wagon.

Harris was on the other end of the semicircle, gun aimed at the motorcycle.

"Hands up!" Harris shouted.

The man was pinned between the motorcycle and the station wagon. His hands slowly went up.

Harris approached swiftly and we joined him.

"Right on time, Detective," I said.

"Consider it a make up for letting you down earlier," he said. He kicked the man's shoe softly and said, "Lift your visor, now!"

Reluctantly, the man lifted the visor of his motorcycle helmet.

A young black man with sharp features stared back at us—striking black eyes, a single lock hanging down on his face through the helmet, and sharp cheeks, as if he were emaciated. His legs was bleeding from where the bike had gashed him.

"Branford Lamar," I said, "you got a lot of explaining to do."

Then he opened his mouth, revealing two fangs, and hissed at me.

"You're making a mistake, necromancer," he said.

Fiona's college boyfriend was a vampire.

CHAPTER TWENTY-ONE

DURING MY LAST ADVENTURE, I learned a little tactic that works whenever you need to extract information from someone: take them to the riverfront and threaten to throw them in unless they tell you what you want to hear. Works wonders, especially if you're scared of water.

Vampires are weak against water. Actually, they're weak against *running* water. It's a purifying force, and they won't go anywhere near it.

Hence, the little tactic I told you about. Now, hear me out. I wasn't going to torture the kid. I wasn't going to throw him in the water. I just wanted information. Harris agreed with me, and we agreed not to do anything crazy.

My dark side was coming out tonight. If your blood and soul were stained, you were racing against the clock to stop a crazy vampire, cautiously awaiting a rogue demon to pop out of nowhere and finish you off, and you couldn't use hardly any of your powers, you'd be a little desperate too.

We drove downtown to the St. Louis Riverfront and parked on a little road that ran parallel to the Mississippi River, right next to the Gateway Arch. The arch was extra reflective tonight, and the Mississippi was flowing fast and heavy. The luminous STL skyline sprawled out in both directions next to the Arch—blue and orange and purple and red against the navy blue sky.

The last time I was here, Visgaroth tried to use the Arch as a portal to access the jinn world. It was nice to not have to save my city's iconic monument tonight.

Cool air rolled off the water, and spotlights crisscrossed the sky on the other side of the river—a bunch of strip clubs in Sauget, Illinois.

"Last chance to start talking," I said as Harris pulled Branford out of his black sedan. Branford wore handcuffs and he limped.

Branford stared daggers at me and didn't say a word. He didn't look the Wash U type. A little rough around the edges and a hateful scowl. However old this kid was, he looked twice his age, both physically and spiritually. The guy was skinny too. Vampirism will do that to you—it destroys every part of you that's human. I bet he had a baby face before he got turned.

"I thought I was making a mistake," I said to Branford. "You might want to retract that statement, young man."

Still staring at me, Branford spit into the grass.

"We're not going to get interrupted, are we?" I asked Harris. "Last time I was here, this didn't go so well. Police and all."

"I've got permission to do what is necessary," Harris said. "Don't worry. I called ahead and forewarned dispatch. I've got the green light to use unorthodox tactics. I have more flexibility in Paranormal Crimes."

"Unorthodox tactics for unorthodox and messed up people," Bo said. He leaned against my Town Car, folding his arms. "Sounds about right." Ant'ny stood next to him, hands dug into his hoodie. Hazel stayed in the car, sticking her head out of the rear driver side window.

"We're going to make this easy," I said. "I ask a question,

you answer. You fail to give me an answer, and you won't like it."

Branford looked away, snarling.

"You're Fiona's boyfriend," I said.

"Was," Branford said.

"Why'd you break up?" I asked.

"Because I turned her into a vampire," Branford said.

"Whoa," Bo said. "What do you call that? Fourth base?"

"Why'd you turn her?" I asked. "She had her whole life ahead of her."

"And I didn't?" Branford asked. "You think I wanted this?"

I paused. I understood not wanting to be turned into a vampire, but vamps usually got over it. I never met a vampire who regretted their origin…until now.

"How long have you been a vampire?" I asked, narrowing my eyes.

"Two years."

"You turned Fiona two years ago," I said. "Who turned you?"

Branford shrugged. "An ex."

Bo put his fist to his mouth and made an announcer's voice. "Folks, if you thought chlamydia was spreading like wildfire on college campuses, wait 'til you get a load of vampirism!"

"I've heard enough," I said, shaking my head. "Now you're going to teach us how to stop Fiona."

A cocky smile spread across Branford's face. "You can't."

"I can't or you don't want me to?" I asked. "Last I checked, the Vampire Collective wasn't exactly happy about her plans. Aren't you supposed to be on my side?"

"What the hell is that?" Branford asked, smirking. "I don't know what you're talking about."

Harris dragged Branford toward the river. When the vampire saw the running water, he pulled back and resisted.

"You better not—" he said.

I shrugged. "Then maybe you ought to start talking."

Harris struggled to handle him by himself, so I helped.

Vampires had super strength, but the motorcycle crash had weakened Branford. I hooked my arm under his and held him tight.

"Vampire collective," I said quietly. "Tell me the truth."

Branford laughed out loud. "You think I care about those old-world clowns?"

We approached the water. The young man struggled against me. Though weakened, he was still strong.

"Throw me in that water and I'll drag you both in with me," Branford said.

"We won't throw you in if you tell us the truth," I said.

As we approached the water, my legs grew weak. I shook it off.

"Get the hell off me!" Branford yelled.

I resisted his tugs, but now my arms grew weak too. I tried to shake it off, but I couldn't. I stared down at the cold, black waters of the Mississippi and I wanted to throw up.

The bite mark on my wrist flared up, like someone stuck a cattle branding arm on it.

I cried out and let go of Branford. He sensed my weakness and landed a hard sucker punch to my forehead.

I stumbled into the grass. The river's gentle burbling magnified in my head and my instinct told me to crawl backward.

Bo flew over me and grabbed Branford.

"Tag team!" Bo said.

"Answer the question," Harris said.

Harris and Bo tripped Branford, bringing his face down to the edge of the water. He screamed again.

"You're telling me the world will be a better place if we keep sucking blood?" Branford asked.

I shook my head.

"Maybe, maybe not," I said. "I don't trust bloodsuckers, but I also don't trust people who try to kill me."

The wind blew, and suddenly, a female voice spoke.

"I agree with that one hundred percent!"

Fiona hovered in the air next to my car, and something held her. From her back sprouted the enormous orange and black wings of a Monarch butterfly, each wing the size of a car. Two human arms secured her by the waist; two other hands rested next to her.

A demon.

Fiona shrugged, adjusting her red leather beret.

"Fee," Branford said. "I've been looking for you."

"Ladies and gentlemen, meet my maker!" Fiona said. "The one who betrayed me two years ago. Give him a round of applause."

"More like a boo," Bo said.

"I was trying to help you out," Branford said. "There are some vampires who support what you're doing. I wanted to show you that by killing this necromancer. He was going to be a blood offering. I wanted you to remember us when you hatch your plan."

Fiona's face hardened. I really, really, really wanted to throw this kid in the river.

"Remember you?" she asked, lifting higher into the sky. "I remember a few things, all right. I remember walking home to your dorm one night. I remember your teeth in my neck after making out with you. I remember you sucking every last drop of blood from me. And now you want me to remember you when I destroy the vampire race?"

"You know what the urge is like," Branford said. "You know I didn't have a choice."

"It had to be me," Fiona said. "I remember that. Your stupid excuses. Well now, it has to be you, huh?"

The demon's butterfly wings flapped faster.

"But for you, I wouldn't be here," she said. "And you don't deserve to exist in the new world I'm creating."

Glitter leaked from the wings in long, sparkling columns.

"You had the honor of being my maker," she said, "and you'll give me the honor of being your unmaker."

The wings flapped furiously, blowing a harsh wind at Branford, knocking Harris away.

Branford screamed as the wings blew a torrential gust at him, knocking him into the Mississippi River. He went under, emerged, arms flailing, and then, he turned into a floating pile of gold dust that floated down the surface of the river, and away.

Fiona touched down. The human hands still held her, but the butterfly wings steadied.

"God, that felt so good," she said.

"You said you wanted to be good," I said. "You can't do that if you rack up a body count."

"This is just the means," Fiona said. "They'll justify the end."

She grinned at me. "Besides, we've got somewhere to be, Lester."

I opened my mouth to reply, but the next thing I knew, Fiona rocketed toward me. Two of the human hands grabbed me by the waist and lifted me into the air. Suddenly, I was next to her as the St. Louis Riverfront spun below me.

"Stop!" Harris cried, aiming his gun at us.

"*You* stop," Fiona said, "Or you'll lose dear old Lester."

We flew under the Arch and into the sky.

Fiona clicked her tongue.

"Lester, Lester, Lester," she said, glancing upon the skyline. "We need to have a little talk."

I tried not to look down as we flew high over the city.

CHAPTER TWENTY-TWO

"What is it that you want?" Fiona asked.

I had no idea where the hell we were. Her demon wings zigged and zagged so much that I lost track of landmarks. St. Louis was a sprawling city spread out over several counties. At night, everything blended together and the city was like a giant circuit board of light.

The demon's human hands secured me by the waist. They moved occasionally, fingers pressing against my stomach.

Next to me, I smelled sweet perfume, like lemons. Fiona looked out over the city as if it was the most mundane thing in the world that she was flying attached to a giant butterfly demon. She almost looked bored.

"I thought I understood you," she said.

The bite mark on my arm burned like hell. I said nothing.

"I thought I knew what you wanted," she said. "But true to form, Lester, you kept me guessing, and you've become a pain in my ass."

"Did you expect anything less?" I asked.

"Not at all, which is why this is turning into an awesome night."

The wings fanned out, and we drifted downward toward a

massive string of orange lights. A vein of cars zipped by in two different directions—a highway. I kept scanning for landmarks, but the city was being stubborn. The demon kept turning just before I could make out something—then I realized it must have been doing it on purpose.

"Who's your demon friend?" I asked.

"Balfouriel," Fiona said. "The butterfly demon of death. You've never worked with her."

"I'd like to keep it that way," I said. "Where are we going?"

"You can't enjoy the beautiful night, can you?" she asked, sighing. "Fine, Lester. Stay uptight."

Silence. The demon did a barrel roll and we turned upside-down for a while before the demon righted itself. Then, we were flying parallel to the highway.

"This is my last chance," Fiona said.

"To convince me to go home?" I asked. "Not on your life."

"My last chance to do something big with my life," she said. "If I succeed, I'll change history. If I fail, I'll be a pile of dust on the Mississippi."

She looked over at me. "The choice is yours."

"You made this problem for yourself," I said. "It's not on me."

"You're the third party," Fiona said. "The one the vampire race has chosen to stop me. They're betting on you. But I want to give you a reason to support me."

She pointed below to a dark patch of woods.

"I told you from the beginning that I don't have to be your enemy," she said. "Now I'll show you."

The demon flapped and relied on a downdraft, bringing us closer to the tree line. The woody patch was a neighborhood. The curvy streets of a subdivision sharpened into view. Faint blue streetlights outlined cars parked on both sides of the street. A lone headlamp tunneled down one lane.

The demon spun, disorienting me again as we dropped.

My stomach lurched into my mouth as the subdivision wheeled under me and balanced like a scale as the demon settled into a straight line—this time, I could see the houses.

It was a typical suburban neighborhood for St. Louis. Ranch houses built in the '50s and '60s, attached garages big enough for one car, short driveways. Tall, mature trees that rustled and swayed in the night. The houses were so close, they might as well have been on top of each other. I didn't know this neighborhood.

The demon spun again, and when it settled into a straight line, I realized just how fast we were moving.

A small backyard flew up to meet us. I closed my eyes and braced for impact, but the demon flapped its wings just in time, buoying us for a second before it touched down. The hands held me tight.

We were a few yards away from a cute white house with black shutters. The lights in the house were turned off. It had a small patio connected to the house where several wicker chairs wrapped around an oval-shaped fire pit. The entire backyard, set off by a wooden privacy fence, was bordered with hostas. A rusted swing set creaked in the night breeze. Next to it, a small vegetable garden.

"Where are we?" I asked.

"Where everything began," Fiona said.

She laughed. "Name one adversary who ever brought you to her home."

The demon let Fiona and me go. We landed on the grass.

Fiona skipped onto the patio like a little girl and threw herself on one of the wicker chairs. She snapped her fingers and Balfouriel flapped over us and stood on the patio with its wings to the house. The wings spread over the home's windows and shifted to a sparkling navy blue. Whoever looked out those windows probably saw an illusion.

Then I saw the demon's black core for the first time. In place of the butterfly's body, the demon watched us with two narrow, opal slits. It didn't have a mouth. Blue fire blazed on the top of the demon's wings, and the demon sent a fireball into the fire pit, setting it ablaze.

"Have a seat," Fiona said.

Reluctantly, I sat in a chair across from Fiona and stared at the cool blue flames burning in the fire pit. Then I looked up and met Fiona's intense gaze.

She sat in the chair with her legs crossed, arms rested on the chair. The corner of her lip pulled into a slight smile.

"What's this all about?" I asked.

"I'm going to level with you," she said. She pointed to the house.

"This is what I lost," she said. "I was born here. I had a peaceful childhood. My dad used to push me on that swing over there."

A tear leaped into her eye.

"I haven't seen my parents since I became a vampire two years ago," she said.

She unfolded a poster from her back pocket and handed it to me.

It was a missing person poster. She was wearing a beret, a white shirt, and overalls. Her picture smiled with regular teeth—no fangs—and she was so innocent and youthful. Vampirism took the edges off her girlishness. Her name was in big blocky letters on the top: Fiona Grimsby.

"Why haven't you come home?" I asked.

"I can't show my face to my mom," Fiona said. "You know the unspoken rules of the supernatural."

It was a rule in the seedy underbelly of the supernatural world that you didn't inadvertently expose yourself to regular people. Vampires only did it when they needed to feed. Nothing was stopping me from walking onto my porch and declaring to the world that I was a necromancer, but it would be a terrible idea. That said, Fiona didn't strike me as a rule follower.

"You've broken enough rules already," I said. "What's another one?"

"I can't see my family," Fiona said. "I might have the urge to feed. Just being around them will attract bad energy. I can't risk putting them in danger."

"Hmm," I said. "I'm not your therapist, but you make a good point."

Fiona turned to the house.

"Do you know how many times I've sat in this backyard, watching my mom and dad? Do you have any idea how much I've cried because I can't see them? I missed my sister's high school graduation. My grandpa died earlier this year and I never got to say goodbye. All my friends in college are starting their lives, getting married, getting dogs."

Her face hardened. "And here I am, hiding in the shadows."

"I'm sorry this happened to you," I said. "I understand where you're coming from. But what do you want me to do about it?"

"When I cure my vampirism," Fiona said, "you know what I'm going to do? I'm going to go to sleep with my shades open for the first time, and I'm going to let the sun wake me up without fear of burning out of existence. I'm going to roll out of bed, stretch, and I'm going to jump in one of my hatchbacks, and I'm going to drive through the misty morning light all the way here. I'm going to park in the driveway, get out, take a big deep breath as I skip up to the front door, put the key in the lock, enter, and say 'Mom, I'm home!' And I'm going to see my mother's and father's faces for the first time in two years and I'm going to cry like a little girl when they hold me and tell me they love me and that everything is going to be okay. Lester, my life will be *normal*. I'll be able to go to the mall, sit by the river, go to a Cardinals game without fear of an urge. I could find a normal boyfriend for a change, get married. I wouldn't need money because I would have the casino. There's the problem of immortality because I'd still live forever and outlast all my friends and family, but I'll worry about that when the time comes."

She leaned forward and clasped her hands. "Lester, did I say anything unreasonable?"

I didn't know what to say. She made a pretty good argument. If I was turned into a vampire against my will, I'd want normalcy too. But I knew better.

"Fiona," I said, "You didn't say anything crazy, but your new so-called life won't exactly be easy. For starters, how much blood are you going to shed so you can go back to normal?"

"As much as required," she said.

"And you don't see a problem with that?"

"You're okay with the status quo," Fiona said. "You like it that innocent people have their lives wrecked."

"I didn't say that," I said. "But as much as your end result sounds beautiful, you're forgetting about all the shadow deals you've done."

I thumbed at the demon. "I don't know your demon buddy over there, but a hunch tells me you owe her something. And whatever you owe, you're going to have to hide it from your family. The life you see in your mind's eye will just be a fantasy. It's not how it will really be."

Fiona looked at me searchingly. She jumped up and circled the patio, arms folded.

"I'm not an idiot," she said.

"There's a little thing called Tanstaarwos that you should be careful of," I said.

"There ain't no such thing as a rendezvous without strings," Fiona said, faking a yawn. "Come on, Lester. That's necromancy 101. Everyone knows that. You think I spent my brainpower learning silly basics? Besides, I was careful with my deals."

"Everyone fools themselves into thinking they were careful," I said. "But the demons always get us in the end."

Fiona stopped. "They haven't gotten you."

"Oh really?" I asked.

Fiona stomped. "Your problem with Visgaroth is that you let him take advantage of you!"

I stood. "If that's what you want to tell yourself, fine. The truth is that I didn't know what I got myself into."

I glanced over at Balfouriel. I didn't like talking about demons in front of them. They had a way of telling their friends.

"I'm smart enough to navigate these shadow deals on my own," Fiona said. "I've done at least a hundred."

"A *hundred* shadow deals?" I asked. "Are you crazy?"

Fiona gave a childish laugh. "I didn't get to finish a world-class college education, Lester, so I used my brainpower to become a student of demons instead. First was Nephasauroth—he gave me the idea for curing vampirism. I only had to kill a few people in exchange for his magic. Then Amalier gave me the magic that powered my driverless hatchbacks. I can thank Visgaroth for fortifying the casino for me. And Balfouriel, well, she's going to be my secret weapon."

The butterfly demon's eyes narrowed to even smaller slits and her body puffed up and down with laughter.

Through her wings, I could see someone looking out the window of Fiona's house. A woman with dark hair. She craned to get a look at the backyard. Whatever she saw, it wasn't us. She disappeared into the darkness of the house.

Fiona walked up to the wing and put her hand on it as if to touch her mother. She watched after the woman for a few seconds.

"I won't repeat the mistakes of necromancers of old," she said. "My future is bright, and no one will take it from me."

She snapped her fingers. A leather bag appeared in one of Balfouriel's hands, and it passed it to Fiona.

"Now it's time to talk about your future," she said, unzipping the bag.

"My future is none of your business," I said.

"I saw the bite marks on your wrist," she said. "Frankly, the Vampire Collective surprised me by soliciting your help. Maybe I can help you with the little problem you have in exchange for you leaving me alone."

She produced a long stick of chalk.

"To prove that I'm not completely evil, this is my act of goodwill to purify you," she said. "Time for another shadow deal."

CHAPTER TWENTY-THREE

IMAGINE my surprise as Fiona drew a magic circle around the fire pit. Her circles were perfect, like she had been doing this forever. All five points of the pentagram in the inner circle aligned.

She set up several candles around the circle and the demon lit them with the blue fire from its wings.

"You going to join me or what?" she asked, finishing up.

I stood on the patio, unable to believe my eyes.

Necromancers don't have a monopoly on demons, but most supernaturals don't bother with them. If you can shoot magic blasts from your hands, use super strength, shift into an animal, turn invisible whenever you want, or cast intense spells, you can solve your own problems. You don't need to owe favors to a demon. Me, on the other hand—I can only do what I do with the help of the dead and demons.

A vampire summoning a demon was rare—I had never heard of it. If I polled my fellow supernatural friends, they probably would have shaken their heads too. Fiona had the power of immortality and super strength—apparently, that wasn't enough.

"I don't have all night, Lester," she said.

I stepped into the outer circle.

"The only thing missing is the salt," she said, "but I can't use that for obvious reasons."

She dragged two wicker chairs into the outer circle. "Time to show you what I've learned."

The last time a youngster showed me their "necromancy skills," it almost got them killed. I wasn't looking forward to this.

"Wandering demons, I send out a beacon of light to you to ask for your help," Fiona said. "Please stop and offer your assistance."

Silence. We stood in the circle as the wind blew.

Fiona repeated her invocation.

The fire crackled, then changed to green as a face with dark eyes appeared in the flames. The eyes were obsidian ovals with no pupils. Its mouth was full of saw teeth. I had never met this demon before.

"It was just a matter of time before I knew I would encounter the precocious vampire girl that everyone has been talking about," the demon said with a female voice.

"Is that what they're calling me now?" Fiona asked. "I've been called worse."

The demon laughed, then settled on me. "A vampire *and* a necromancer. Tonight must be my lucky night. Some wonders never cease."

I said nothing. If you didn't want to do a deal with a demon, you told them to go away. In my case, I didn't want to reveal anything about myself that could be used against me.

"I need a favor for my companion here," Fiona said. "Let's get a few details out of the way. This is a one-time deal, and I'll put an unlimited time limit on the return payment. I would prefer that you cash in your favor *after* tonight. Accept the terms or go away."

The demon regarded the terms. "I accept your offer. How may I be of assistance?"

"My companion was stained with the blood of a vampire," Fiona said. "I want to know how to purify his blood so he can return to necromancy."

I glanced at Fiona suspiciously. The fire gleamed in her bulbous sunglasses. Why was she so keen on helping me all of a sudden?

The fire crackled as the demon thought about the conundrum.

"This is a complicated problem that does not have an easy solution," the demon said.

No demon I've ever met has ever proposed a simple solution to a problem. They always made things more complicated because they benefited from chaos.

"Well?" Fiona asked.

"This man's soul was indelibly stained," the demon said. "Are you sure you wish to fight for him?"

"I'm positive," Fiona said.

"A vampire defending a necromancer," the demon said. "A new legend is born."

The demon stared me in the eyes and gave me a sawtooth grin. My heart raced.

"If you wish to purify this necromancer's blood," the demon said, "then you must kill him."

CHAPTER TWENTY-FOUR

I BACKED away from Fiona as the demon laughed maniacally.

My foot hit the edge of the outer circle. I couldn't move any further. I wouldn't be able to take Fiona in the circle. I was a sitting duck.

But Fiona didn't take her eyes off the demon.

"Of course I can kill him," she said matter-of-factly. "But what about after?"

"His blood cannot be purified," the demon said. "It is stained beyond repair."

"So you'd rather send me to the spirit world, huh?" I asked, not able to help myself. "That's real rich, demon."

"The only way to purify your blood is to obtain new blood," the demon said. "Blood that is untainted with the marks of sin."

"You're saying I have to kill someone," Fiona said. I could see her brain working hard through her sunglasses. She glanced over at me. "I can totally do that. Any suggestions, Lester?"

"You're not going to kill anyone on my behalf," I said, "even if it's to save my life."

Fiona stomped her foot again. "Quit being stubborn! Can't you see that I'm doing you a favor?"

"It's not a favor," I said. "No matter how you bend this situation into pretzels to make it fit your rosy view of the future, it won't turn out that way."

I gestured to Balfouriel. "Keep making these deals, Fiona, and you're going to regret it."

Fiona puffed. "No suggestions, then. That means I'll choose someone for you."

She tapped her chin with her finger. "Hmm…it can't be anyone you know. That would defeat the purpose. We'll just have to pick a random person's night to ruin, won't we?"

I couldn't let Fiona shed more blood on my account. My mind raced to find a way to stop the sacrifice.

I turned to the demon.

"I refuse to let her kill another human being on my behalf," I said. "If she tries to ink a deal with you, I will reject it."

"Reject!" the demon roared. "To reject means to ensure your death, necromancer."

The demon grew bigger in the flames, rising as tall as me.

"Don't ruin this, Lester," Fiona said.

"No death," I said. "I'll die before I let you sow more discord in the world."

"No, you won't," Fiona said.

"Watch me," I said.

"No, you *won't*," Fiona said. "In my family, you don't kick a gift horse in the mouth."

"I've never met a gift horse," I said, "but if it looked like you, I wouldn't have a problem doing damage."

Fiona balled her fists and shouted.

"No, no, no!"

"You heard me, demon," I said. "No death."

The demon crackled in anger. "I acknowledge your demand."

"Then tell me a way around it," Fiona said. "If he doesn't want death, tell me another way."

The demon shook its head. "There is no other way."

"Lester, you're destroying my night," Fiona said. "Demon, do not forget my offer, as it still stands."

The demon nodded.

"Go away," she said.

A sudden gust blew, fanning the fire. The demon closed its eyes as the fire swelled, and then decreased to a faint ember in the fire pit. Silence settled in across the backyard.

I scuffed out a portion of the inner magic circle with my foot and stepped out.

"You idiot," Fiona said, standing, staring at the fire pit. She didn't look at me. "I tried to save your life and you wouldn't let me."

"You didn't give me any other choice," I said. "If you knew anything about me, you'd know I don't stand for innocent people dying."

"The ends justify the means," Fiona said. A sly smile crept across her face. It sent chills down my spine.

Fiona waved a hand. Balfouriel sent a wave of fire from its wings, eradicating the magic circle. She replaced the wicker chairs to their original position before we landed in the backyard.

"If you won't let people die, then I guess people are going to have to die," she said.

She snapped her fingers. Balfouriel dashed into the air, its wings flapping furiously. Its human hands grabbed Fiona, and then the butterfly demon made a sharp turn and grabbed me.

"Where are we going?" I asked.

"To your new place of regret," Fiona said.

The wind whipped around us as the demon bulleted up into the sky again.

CHAPTER TWENTY-FIVE

Balfouriel sped through the sky like a ballistic missile, covered in flames. The demon kept spinning too, disorienting me. I couldn't see through the flames.

Fiona settled into the demon's arms next to me. I felt her warmth. The demon's heat was so hot and it moved so fast, it was difficult to hear. Worked for me—I didn't exactly feel like talking to her after what she put me through.

Balfouriel dipped and my stomach dropped as we spiraled down toward a giant building shaped like a T.

The demon's wings glowed as they wrapped over me. Through the wing's speckled membranes, the lights of the city flew by in frosted glass, spinning around madly as Balfouriel turned.

I put my arms in front of my eyes to protect myself from the flames as the demon scooped the ground. Concrete whirled up below me, inches away from my nose. Then the butterfly pulled up, hovered, and slammed down.

It let go of me and I rolled to the ground along with Fiona.

Balfouriel's wings flashed as they clicked and expanded

like a socket wrench. The next thing I knew, Fiona and I were enclosed in a circular wall of wing on all sides. The demon's slitted eyes burned with blue fire as it stared at Fiona, waiting for instructions.

"Let us see out," Fiona said, waving a hand.

The wings' frosted texture changed to transparent.

We were in an outdoor shopping mall. I had no idea where. We were in the middle of a courtyard next to a fountain with a clay Clydesdale horse. Water gushed around the horse in geyser-like jets with LEDs changing the water color every few seconds.

People passed around us. Men, women, and children with shopping bags. Somewhere, rock and roll music played—probably from a bar. The people walked by as if they didn't see a giant butterfly demon in the middle of the walkway. Balfouriel's wings made us invisible.

The mall buildings were department stores, restaurants, and bars with outdoor seating.

"Where are we?" I asked.

"The place of your destiny," Fiona said.

One of Balfouriel's hands passed her the leather kit.

"Bal, amend our deal," Fiona said flatly.

She stuck out her finger, held it up in the air, and closed her eyes. Then she stuck out her tongue, showing a fang, and she spun around wildly. I jumped out of the way as she almost bumped into me.

"Whooooooa," she said, "who will we choose? Maybe I'll stop now…maybe I'll stop now…NOW!"

She stopped and flicked her wrist down to a bar and grill across from Balfouriel. People were eating barbecue at metal patio tables under a corrugated metal overhang.

"Here we go!" she said, pointing to the tables. "Kill them all."

My eyes widened.

"I told you no killing!" I cried.

But it was too late. Purple energy oozed from the butterfly demon's wings and floated across the bar like smoke. No one noticed it.

I threw myself against the glass, but the demon's wings wouldn't budge.

Fiona laughed.

"I only promised not to kill people to purify you," she said. "We're not doing a deal right now. I can kill anyone I damn well please."

A woman sitting alone at a table face-planted into a plate of ribs.

"Stop," I said.

"Not yet, Lester," Fiona said. She joined me at the glass. "If you listen closely, you might be able to hear their hearts stopping. It's not too late for them, though."

One by one, patrons at the tables dropped. The purple cloud grew bigger and bubbles formed inside it.

"Stop!" I cried.

"Isn't it amazing?" Fiona asked. "People are dying because you're so damned stubborn, Lester."

Passersby stopped and started screaming and pointing at the people in the restaurant who were dropping left and right.

Fiona shrugged. "But there is a way to save them, isn't there?"

Another person fell out of their chair and onto the floor, staring at me with their eyes open. Their breathing slowed.

"I guess you'll have to do a bunch of shadow deals to get these people back," she said. "That is, if the reapers will let you. Will they?"

She folded her arms and paced around, dragging a finger against the glass.

"They're going to die any minute now, Lester. Their blood will be on your hands, but it didn't have to be this way. But you can save them if you want."

A waterfall of a shadow appeared just outside the demon's wings. I recognized it as a reaper.

"Hey," I cried, beating the glass. "This is foul play!"

The reaper ignored me. It palmed a gold coin that turned into an electric blue scythe. It crouched, waiting.

I dropped to my knees.

"If you want them to live, you'll have to live," Fiona said. "If they die, you can join them in the afterlife and explain how you were responsible for their deaths."

"No," I said under my breath.

Everyone on the restaurant patio was on the floor now, unresponsive. Bystanders were on the floor, providing assistance and CPR. A siren sounded far away.

"Say it," Fiona said. "Say the words you should have said in my backyard."

I gulped. My stomach churned and I was going to be sick.

"You win," I said quietly.

Fiona held up a hand. She put a hand on my shoulder, but I shrugged it off.

"Good decision," she said.

One of Balfouriel's hands passed her the leather kit. Fiona quickly scrawled a magic circle and called for a demon.

The glass shimmered and the demon from the backyard appeared in Balfouriel's wing, obsidian eyes staring at me.

"Tell him you're reneging your prior comments," Fiona said. "No bullshit!"

"I take back what I said," I said.

The demon laughed. "She didn't take long to work on you."

"Leave these people alone," I said. "Now!"

Fiona held up a hand and tilted her head at Balfouriel.

The purple energy around the bar faded. Slowly, the restaurant patrons began breathing again. I watched them with bated breath as each person stood up, looking around in a daze as if they had been drugged. My heart sank. These people would carry this moment with them for the rest of their lives. They'd always remember what it felt like to be on the cold patio floor, staring at nothing at all, on the verge of death as their organs shut down. Worse, no one would ever have an explanation for them why it happened.

"Thanks, Lester," Fiona said. "You saved your life tonight, but you also helped me fulfill a prior deal."

I hung my head and balled my fists.

"I made a deal with a twin-headed demon that I'd increase the misery in the city by scarring at least fifteen people," Fiona said. "I'm counting at least thirty people on this patio, so that should be enough to get those annoying demons off my back."

"Everything is about deals to you," I said. "You have no regard for people's lives."

"Of course I do," Fiona said. "Thirty people are alive today because you had mercy."

"Mercy!" I cried, rising to my feet. "You're playing with people like pawns. These demons are doing the same with you. Heaven help you on the day you discover the painful truth about what you've really been doing to yourself."

Fiona smirked. "Oooh, you're telling me I'm going to rue this day, huh? Let's handshake on it. If I ever regret this, you can have your smug self-satisfaction. But what if you're wrong?"

She paused.

"What if it turns out that I was right?" she asked.

"You're not right," I said.

"But what if I AM?" Fiona said, exploding. "What would you do, Lester?"

She approached me. "You wouldn't know what to do with yourself."

I stood my ground.

"Everything you ever fought for would have been a lie," she said. "And your notions of good and evil would be wrong. You would have to acknowledge that my way is better and more realistic."

She laughed, extending a hand. "Let's shake on it."

I stared at her.

"Let it be known today that there are two types of necromancy," she said. "The first is your type, the subtle type. The second is the one I will be known for—necromancy by force, and by demons, accomplished by those with iron wills."

"You can't approach necromancy like you approach the vampire life," I said. "You just throw your power around, but you don't know what the consequences will be. That's why restraint is always better."

"Restraint!" Fiona asked. "If I practiced restraint, I'd still be sucking blood tomorrow."

"Fiona, why are you trying to save me?" I asked.

"Who else can spar with me intellectually and supernaturally?" she asked. "Everyone else in the supernatural world is so boooooring. But you and me—we'll soon be equals. Let's see about our debate, shall we?"

She wiggled her hand to let me know it was still there. I took it and pumped, gazing into her crazed eyes.

"Now, just sit back and let the ritual take its course," she said. "I'll pick someone at random to purify your blood."

She produced a knife from her back pants pocket.

My eyes widened.

"Time for a renaissance, Lester," Fiona said.

She thrust the knife at my gut, but just before it struck my skin, a hand grabbed me and pulled me aside.

Fiona missed and struck the glass, knocking the knife out of her hands.

"Aaagh!" she cried.

A giant cobalt blue hand had locked around my waist.

"What the—" I said.

Fiona dove for the knife, broke into a run, and leaped into the air, her fangs bared.

"You won't rob me of this!" she cried.

The hand dragged me backward, and shadows enveloped me. The last thing I saw before they covered my eyes completely was Fiona slashing and screaming at me.

CHAPTER TWENTY-SIX

A‍ll I could see was darkness. Shadows flowed past me like gentle air.

The hand around my waist held me tight. I closed my eyes.

Maybe Fiona had killed me and this hand was taking me to the great beyond. It wouldn't have surprised me, but I knew what death was. Death was the cold hands of a reaper.

This hand—it wasn't a reaper.

I guess it didn't matter now. I had to go wherever it was taking me, and I didn't have to listen to Fiona's crazy voice for the first time in a while.

Intense light shone against my eyelids, making me open them. The hand dragged me toward a blazing white corona of light in the distance. I put my hands in front of my face as it pulled me into it.

The next thing I knew, I was looking up at the stars. A melody of cricket song and river rush drowned out the darkness.

I lay on a soft surface.

A voice spoke to me.

"Boss man, you all right?"

Bo. He took my hand and helped me sit up.

Tan metal caught my eye—my car.

I was sitting on top of my '93 Lincoln Town Car.

"What happened?" I asked as I slid down onto asphalt.

"Long story," Bo said, "but it looks like we got you just in time."

I looked around. We were still at the St. Louis Riverfront, but my car was on the frontage road that ran along the Mississippi River. The Arch glimmered behind us.

On the road circling my car was…chalk. A magic circle. My car was in an enormous inner ring. Harris, Ant'ny, and Hazel sat in the outer ring. I waved at them.

"We broke the circle safely," Bo said.

I put my hands on my hips and stared at the sight—my car in the middle of the street, in the middle of a magic circle. I would have loved to see the face of the first person who drove by.

"Harris did a shadow deal to save you," Bo said.

"But we couldn't perform necromancy," I said, my mind racing.

"Natkaal is gone," Harris said. "And no one said that *I* couldn't use necromancy. We made a magic circle and I called a demon. I asked for it to find you and bring you back."

I didn't want to think about what Harris would have to do in return for the demon that saved me. But I appreciated it and offered my hand. Harris shook it.

"Where the hell did Fiona take you?" Harris asked.

"She took me to her home," I said, shaking my head. "She's crazier than I thought. She offered to purify my blood to remove the stain."

"Why would she do that?" Bo asked, scratching his head.

I shrugged. "But she insisted on saving me. Made me an offer I couldn't refuse."

"So you're cured now?" Bo asked.

"The purification involved killing me first and then

replacing my blood with someone else's. You saved me before she struck me with the knife."

"Oh," Bo said. "Well, damn."

"I can't get a handle on her," I said. "Every time I meet her, I come away more confused. But I know one thing: if we go to the casino, she'll be there. That's where everything is going to go down."

I glanced down the river toward the casino. A lone bat darted out of a tree and into the sky, flying along the river.

I didn't know what I was going to find at the casino, but I knew there was only one thing left to do.

"Let's ride," I said.

We packed into my car, Ant'ny, Hazel, and Harris in the backseat. Bo reversed the car and sped down the river road.

We passed under the Eads Bridge. The streetlights on the historic steel and stone bridge zoomed by overhead as we passed under Roman coliseum-like tunnels that covered the roadway. A column of ragged darkness broke off the bottom of the bridge and followed us, swooshing past the windshield and into the night sky.

More bats.

"They're leading the way," Bo said. "Paint me blue and call me Kentucky."

Thank God we had a cop in the car with us because Bo was pushing sixty. We were a little too close to the river for my liking; my wrist swelled and burned, and I grabbed it out of habit. When Bo turned off the river road up a small commercial street that took us away from the Mississippi, the pain subsided and I relaxed a little.

Bo cut through empty streets and took a quick right. The Chateau Casino rose into the sky, its neon pink frame glowing in the night. The front parking lot was packed and a line of cars waited in front of the hotel's porte-cochere.

The bats circled up to the roof and then away over the

rooftops. A massive bolt of lightning struck the roof, even though there were no clouds in the sky.

"Whoa, damn!" Ant'ny said, pointing at the roof.

"What is it?" I asked.

"That vampire we saw earlier had butterfly wings, right?" he asked.

"She's working with a butterfly demon," I said.

"There are giant wings up there," Ant'ny said. "On the roof."

"I don't see nothin'," Bo said, craning to get a better look.

"Trust me," Ant'ny said. "She's up there."

"Fiona is waiting for us, then," I said as Bo careened into the parking lot.

CHAPTER TWENTY-SEVEN

THE OLDER I GET, the more I appreciate the quiet life. When you have enough nights like the one I was having—where innocent people's lives were needlessly at stake, my neighbor's third eye was open, and I somehow narrowly avoided death—you suddenly want a vacation. You want to get in your car and drive like hell as far away from home and to nowhere in particular. You want to park your car at a hotel, throw your keys at the valet attendant, and tell 'em you don't care if you ever see the damn car again because you're staying as long as you want and you don't need keys. At least, that was how I liked to romanticize what I was going to do when this night was over.

The valets in front of the casino looked at us in the same way I imagined they would in my daydreams as we left my car parked in the middle of a busy valet line. We didn't have time to wait and there was no way in hell you were going to get me in that parking garage again. Tall glass of nope on that.

Ironically, the casino and hotel we were running into was exactly the kind of place I might have wanted to disappear to on a runaway vacation: a three-star resort with a casino and battery of fancy restaurants on the bottom, and a Four

Seasons hotel on top. Rather, I should say, *what used* to be a casino, a gaggle of restaurants, and a hotel. There was no telling what Fiona had done with the place.

It certainly looked like the place I frequented. Dark carpet, ultra-modern chandeliers, wide-open lobby leading into an indoor atrium with hotel suites looking down on it. The only difference was the bats.

Someone screamed as we ran through the atrium. The bats flew ahead of us and up, up, up to the top floor. The bats wouldn't stop streaming in—an entire river of them flowed to the top level of the hotel. I wish I could have taken a picture of people's faces as the elevator doors closed and we rocketed to the top floor.

The elevator doors opened into the same hallway from before—the private suites. The flesh-colored walls with red lines pulsing through like veins guided us forward. This time, instead of walking to the door to Fiona's suite, we followed the bats to the other end of the dark hallway, up a short set of steps, and through a glass door that led to a rooftop pool. The bats flashed through the glass as if it were nothing.

A rectangular pool was lit up in hues of yellow, surrounded by beach cabanas. The Arch shimmered in the distance.

Fiona lounged in one of the cabanas facing the pool, drinking a glass of wine. Her legs were crossed. The bats amassed into a huge pillar on the other side of the pool. The bats shrieked at her.

"Shut up," she said to the bats. "You're completely irrelevant and no one is going to have any sympathy for you when I'm done."

"Fiona," I said. "This ends now."

"There he is," she said, raising her glass to me. "The man who escapes death!"

She took a sip and rose, surveying us. Several shadows

emerged from behind the cabana. Her vampires. At least a dozen of them.

"Clever shadow deal," she said, nodding to Harris. "What did you have to sacrifice to save him?"

"None of your business," Harris said. "Fiona, stop right there. Tell me what you've done with the five people who went missing from the hotel management."

Fiona dangled her wine glass. "And if I don't?"

"I'm placing you under arrest," Harris said, drawing his gun.

"Missing people?" she asked, tapping her finger against her chin. "You're asking the difficult questions tonight, Detective. Which ones again?"

She smirked, and I knew more bullshit was coming.

"Were they the ones I drowned?" she asked. "No, that was in Illinois. Oh! Wait! I did decapitate five people—you can thank good ol' Visgaroth for that. Messy business, but it helped my plans. No, wasn't them. Maybe the last five people I fed on? Yes, that's right—one of them was in a hotel…but hotel management? You're stumping me, Detective. I've killed so many!"

She held out her palms, the wine in her glass swirling. "No wonder I didn't remember them off the top of my head. That's because I didn't kill them yet!"

She snapped her fingers. In a sparkle of light, several people in gray uniforms appeared in the cabana. They were tied up, and sleeping.

"My human engines," she said.

I started toward the cabana, but Bo held me back.

"None of this would be possible without human sacrifice," Fiona said. "You have no idea how many deals I had to do to keep these people in perpetual sleep."

"Why do you need them?" I asked. "These are innocent people. They have families, Fiona."

"Haven't you ever heard of Turzoth's rules?" Fiona asked.

"If you want to cast a spell, then you should mirror the numerology of your intended target. Five is such a human number, isn't it? Five fingers, five toes—it doesn't get any more symbolic than that. Plus, to do what I'm going to do, there has to be a death of innocents. It's just part of the game, Lester."

She leaned over one of the sleeping bodies—a middle-aged man with graying hair and a goatee. The guy was sleeping like a baby. "I need five pure and innocent people to sacrifice to advance to the next phase of my life. I'm just doing what I was told."

"This isn't going to work out for you," I said.

"What isn't going to work out?" Fiona asked. "I've planned it so perfectly. A hundred shadow deals led me here. How many deals have *you* done, Lester? At some point, your deals pick up critical mass and start working magic for you."

She held out her hands, gesturing to the Arch. "The city will worship me like I'm meant to be worshipped. And the best part? They won't even know it."

"I said it before and I'll say it again: you're a crazy chick," Bo said. "You may be a vampire, but you ain't no goddess."

"Tell me what you think in five minutes," she said. She balled her fist and did an excited dance. "Oh, I just LOVE the numerology tonight!"

"I said freeze," Harris said, approaching her. "Hands up."

"You know that bullets only slow me down," Fiona said.

"Final warning," Harris said, locking on her.

Fiona ignored him and produced her leather kit from the cabana.

Harris fired at her, but a lane of glass slashed down and blocked the bullet, making it drop to the ground in a heated blaze.

One of Balfouriel's wings appeared out of nowhere. Suddenly, the butterfly demon had formed a protective circle around her.

In her new safety, Fiona drew a magic circle. The demon followed her as she created another. And another. Five total.

I wasn't going to let her win. Call me crazy, but I didn't want to be beaten at my own game.

"Harris," I said. "Draw a magic circle on the other side of the pool."

I pulled out my own leather kit with chalk, candles, and a lighter. I tossed him a stick of chalk.

"You sure about this?" Harris asked.

"I'm sure," I said. "Listen to me closely."

Together, we scrabbled magic circles on both sides of the pool. Then I told him to drew another.

I drew a fifth circle.

Soon, Harris and I each stood in a circle on separate sides of the pool. I motioned Bo and Ant'ny to each take a circle behind Harris. There was one empty circle next to me.

"Oooh, the Good Necromancer is getting complicated!" Fiona said.

We were in a magic circle showdown.

"Let the demon games begin!" Fiona shouted.

CHAPTER TWENTY-EIGHT

If you've gotten this far and know *anything* about me, you know that I don't like demons. I don't like talking to them, I don't like doing deals with them, and I especially don't like summoning them to do my bidding. I put up with them because they're a part of the dark arts. Kind of like your annoying uncle. It's just a fact of life that your Uncle Rosco is going to say or do something stupid at Thanksgiving and you're going to have to put on your best smile and pass the cranberry sauce. The same is true with demons—when you go searching for dead people to talk to for information, you're going to run into a demon or two. Some of them treat necromancy as transactional—they don't ask for much with a shadow deal. Others will try to ruin your life, force you to break your magic circle, or even possess you. Some try to do all three at the same time.

So why, Lester, would you create not one, but *five* magic circles to summon five demons? Because I had to show this youngster what the dark arts were really about.

Fiona called a demon into her circle. The demon from earlier appeared, a translucent silhouette with obsidian eyes and a mouth full of saw teeth.

She pointed at me. "Our deal still stands."

I closed my eyes and called for a demon. "Wandering demons, I send out a beacon of light to you to ask for your help. Please stop and offer your assistance."

A breeze blew. A swirling pillar of shadow appeared in my inner magic circle.

"Necromancer versus vampire," the shadow said.

"Quick deal," I said. "Whatever she and her demon do, I need you to nullify their spell."

The shadow pillar regarded Fiona and the demon.

"I cannot complete this deal without knowing what their spell will be," the demon said.

"Then we'll leave the door open," I said. "Let's talk after we see what they do."

"Very well," the pillar said.

"The first step to my plan is to clean the wounds that the vampire race has created," Fiona said.

She waved her hand.

The demon locked its gaze on the ragged column of bats. An invisible force dragged the column of bats into my empty magic circle. A wall of light shimmered around them. The bats shrieked.

My heart sank. Fiona had made a boss move and I didn't have my pawns into formation yet. I didn't expect her to use my empty circle.

"I cannot move something out of a magic circle," the demon said. "Items can only be moved in."

Fiona laughed. "Oops, Lester!"

"Fine," I said. "Then destroy the circle."

Fiona's face changed to anger as the demon waved a shadowy hand, scribbling the magic circle out of existence. The bat column broke apart, flew off the roof, and curved around in a long wand as they zoomed back toward us.

"I can play that too!" Fiona said, pointing at my circle.

Suddenly, it began to disappear.

"Be gone," I said quickly to the demon for fear of Fiona breaking my circle and releasing it. The demon disappeared in a puff of smoke just as my circle disappeared.

Harris stood, watching intently. I trusted him to make a good move. I had one circle left. Two if I counted Harris's.

"Contain the bats!" Fiona cried. "And kill Lester."

I had to get to my magic circle, fast. I started running. Outside of it, I had no protection.

The demon silhouette scanned the sky as the bats cascaded across the rooftop, this time blanketing the air over the pool.

I ran toward the remaining circle on my side, but my bite marks flared up and the bats slammed into me.

I flew through the air and landed in the pool headfirst. The cool, ever-changing LED lights of the water pulsed and the emerald tiles on the pool floor glinted as I plunged into the warm water. On any other night, it might have felt amazing to go for a swim.

Thank God I *knew* how to swim. I used to do a few laps at the YMCA every week. I kicked my legs and swam up to the surface with strong, long strokes. Time seemed to slow down underwater, and what took me seconds to climb to felt like minutes.

I broke the water, gasping for air.

I spun around, treading water and looking for Fiona.

I wasn't on the hotel rooftop anymore.

I was floating in a dark cavern with torches on the walls. Knobby stalactites hung from the ceiling.

Below me, the hotel pool still pulsed colors and rippled gently.

The cave was eerily silent aside from my arms splashing through the water.

"Where am I?" I asked, swimming to the edge of the pool. I pulled myself out of the water and onto a cold, rocky floor.

"Advance, Lester," a faint voice said. I knew from the

hard-to-place, androgynous tone that it was the Vampire Collective.

Several yards away, a torchlit hallway crackled. I crossed into the hallway, dripping with water. I had to crouch because it was so low.

I emerged back into the stone room I'd seen before—a dais with a pine coffin on it. My name was engraved on the lid.

I gulped.

"We do not have much time, Lester," the Vampire Collective said. "Our time to strike is now."

"What's the plan?" I asked.

"Get in," the Vampire Collective said. "We will finish Fiona off with a powerful spell."

I climbed onto the dais and into the coffin. I lay down, my clothes squishing as I got comfortable.

The lid floated up and slammed onto the coffin.

I rested my hands on my chest and closed my eyes. Immediately, the bottom of the coffin dropped away and I fell into deeper darkness.

A brilliant aurora danced across my eyelids.

"Hold out your left hand," the voice said.

"What are you making me do?" I asked.

"There is no time for talking," the collective said. "We are in position."

I paused. "It would help if I knew what the plan was."

"You will know intrinsically when it is time," the collective said hastily. "Hold out your hand, Lester!"

I don't know why I got the urge to open my eyes. You know how sometimes you need to trust, but verify?

I opened my eyes and beheld a giant, swirling face of red energy. To call it a face was a compliment—it was pockmarked with a slanted mouth that made a W. Its white irises were bleeding, and blood leaked down its cheeks like never-ending tears. Fangs curved down its mouth like a sabretooth tiger. It howled with rage upon me seeing it.

"You were instructed to keep your eyes closed!" the collective shouted, turning its face away.

A serrated knife hovered next to me. It glowed orange.

"Take the knife," the collective said quickly. "Our fate rests in your hands."

"I can't do anything with a knife," I said. "Why are you giving this to me?"

"To kill Fiona requires a blood sacrifice," the collective said.

I arched an eyebrow. "So that's what this is about?" I asked. "You were using me. That's why you wanted a third party, so you could keep your hands clean?"

"Your sacrifice will not be in vain," the collective said. "If you do not die, then Fiona will win."

CHAPTER TWENTY-NINE

To say that I didn't want to take the serrated knife offered to me by the Vampire Collective was an understatement. To say that I wanted Fiona to kill me was a *gross* understatement.

"If you do not act," the Vampire Collective said, "we will die, and so will you, your dog, and your servant."

"My servant's already dead," I said.

The Vampire Collective swirled into anger, growing bigger.

"Then you must decide if sacrificing your own life and the lives of two you love are worth defiance," the collective said.

My stomach knotted at the thought of Hazel dying and Bo being released into the spirit world. We would both be spirits.

"You vampires love your blood sacrifices," I said. "Maybe we can talk more about how foolish you are when I'm in the great beyond."

The collective's eyes widened in horror.

"You will *not* defy us!" it cried. "If you allow us to perish, you don't know what suffering you will bring upon the world!"

Did I want to die? Nope. But was I going to let this collective use me like a pawn? My mama didn't raise no punk.

"Help me understand the suffering," I said. "People won't

have to worry about walking down a street in the middle of the night and get bitten by a vampire. I'd say that's a win for humanity."

"No!" the collective cried.

"If you want me to sacrifice myself so much," I said, "why don't you drive the knife in yourself?"

The collective could influence me, but it couldn't make me take action. If they could have, they would have. If I was going to sacrifice myself, *I* had to be the one to do it. That meant I had all the leverage. I had to keep stalling.

"How about you let me out of this chamber and we see how this turns out?" I asked.

"We will infect everyone in your neighborhood," the collective said. "The casualty number will be much higher."

"You know, if you had asked me nicely and explained how crazy Fiona was, maybe I would have worked with you," I said, knowing damn well it was a lie.

The serrated knife rotated around my head like a planet in orbit.

I floated there in the darkness, not taking my eyes off the collective. I stared the amalgamation straight in the eyes. I wanted it to know that I meant business.

Was I ready to die? No one ever is.

"Tell me something," I said. "If you were so worried about Fiona, why didn't you attack her yourselves? Why a third party?"

"The girl cobbled her plans together too quickly," the collective said. "This building is filled with traps that would be mortal to full-blooded vampires. Her shadow deals ensured that. We needed someone who could bypass them."

The vampire race was in so much danger that its collective conscience tried to save it. That's how desperate it was. If they were desperate, then I could be desperate too.

I don't want to make it seem like I'm cavalier about death. I take my mortality seriously. But I've got a beautiful wife, an amazing son, a lich friend, and thousands of ancestors who will welcome me with open arms. You don't have to weep for me when I'm gone. I did some evil in this world, but I like to think I did enough good to cancel it out. I just hope I had enough tallies to the good in the celestial heavens.

"So you've chosen against your best interests," the collective said.

"I choose humanity," I said. "Even if I won't be among it."

Then, the darkness around me burst into water, washing the collective's face away into a bloody swirl.

I inhaled, but took in warm, chlorinated water into my nose. Suddenly, I was back in the pool, struggling with my arms and legs flailing.

A pair of hands pulled me out of the water and I gasped. The hotel rooftop spun around as Bo laid me across a cabana bed.

I coughed up water as Bo's face hovered over me.

Bo.

He was outside of his magic circle. He wasn't following instructions. Hazel was next to him, whimpering.

Slowly, I came to.

I reached a hand and nuzzled Hazel's neck.

"You were supposed to stay in your circle," I said.

"Ride or die, boss man," Bo said. "I knew something was afoot when the pool turned into a giant cave and you disappeared inside it. Ant'ny told us what was up. We could only see a giant cavern, but it was just an illusion. Once we saw it, the cave disappeared and you were floating on the edge of the water."

Outside, Harris stood in his magic circle, calling a demon. The pool was riddled with bats floating on the surface of the water.

Wham!

Harris went flying and slammed against the wall of the hotel.

The translucent demon laughed. Harris's magic circle dissolved.

There were no magic circles around the pool now. Fiona stood in her circle, surveying the damage.

I stumbled off the cabana and ran to the pool, facing her.

The truth was that I didn't know what I was going to do. I had no plan, no strategy, and I could barely breathe.

Each of Fiona's inner circles contained a demon, each a different kind of insect-human hybrid. They held the five innocent sleeping people in their arms.

Something crashed into me, knocking me to the ground. Two rows of sharp, yellow saw teeth stared me down.

"I told you I'd find and kill you, Lester Broussard!"

Natkaal grinned as he pinned me down. The grasshopper demon's papery face was ready to tear me up. The demon had literally come out of nowhere. Something warm dripped on my leg—blue blood from where the Venus flytrap had torn one of its legs off. The blood sizzled on my pants leg.

"I'm already toast, Natkaal," I said.

"Just in time for me to rip you apart, then!" he cried.

Fiona raised her hand upon seeing me, and she flicked her wrist. The demons began to chant. Their voices started slow and harsh, but they crescendoed. The syllables clashed against each other, making me want to cover my ears.

Lightning struck the pool, electrifying it with sparks. The bats shrieked as electricity fried them. The smell of burnt flesh covered the rooftop.

Natkaal looked over at the dead bats and the demon's eyes widened.

Fiona's vampires cheered.

"I delivered, team!" Fiona said, grinning. "But I have bad news for you."

Lightning bolts struck Fiona's team of vampires, rendering

them to instant dust. Their screams ripped across the rooftop, cut short by their transformation to dust.

Fiona shrugged. "I only negotiated one cure in the deals."

"How high will your body count go?" I asked angrily.

"Yo, look!" Ant'ny cried, pointing at the city skyline.

All over the city, lightning bolts struck out of a clear sky. The combined screams of vampires gathered all over the city, rose on the wind, and then faded as quickly as they came. I swore I saw pillars of steam rising from various parts of the skyline.

A sharp pain surged through my body like I had been struck with electricity too. I was jelly under the giant grasshopper demon's weight.

Bo collapsed and Hazel fell onto the ground too.

So this was how it was going to go down, I thought as the electricity cut through me.

"What is this madness?" Natkaal asked, screwing up his face.

A fierce wind crashed into the demon, knocking him off me.

"Take a number, demon!" Fiona cried.

The next thing I saw was Fiona in the air, blade in her hand, flying down at me.

The knife pierced my stomach and my body convulsed twice before lying on the cement, bleeding out.

The last thing I saw was Fiona twisting the knife.

CHAPTER THIRTY

IN CASE YOU WERE WONDERING, here's what happens when you die: any pain you feel on the threshold of death pops, and then you don't feel anything.

You float, and you don't leave the place you died. Not right away. Your soul flashes over your body and you're exactly where you died, but you don't see it the same way. Everything is muted in a gray haze. Your sense of perception is warped, and you only perceive what needs to be perceived—for the dead, they don't need to see details because they can see the essence of things. Whether or not someone is wearing a blue shirt has nothing to do with the greater scheme of the universe. What matters is how they *are*.

And, of course, you wait around for a reaper, which isn't long. Within seconds of your death, you're staring at a shadowed figure with a pale face, and it curls a bony finger at you to come hither. The finger curl is a trick. If you agree, it will clap blue electric handcuffs on you and you will be tied to the reaper until it delivers you to the spirit world, and you will receive bonus points for cooperation when it turns you over to the lich who will eventually preside over your soul. Do enough good behavior and you'll eventually transcend to the next plane of existence. If you refuse the reaper's demand, it will trap you all the same. They don't permit fugitives.

As far as I know, no soul has *ever* escaped from a reaper, and I wasn't about to experiment to see if I could be the first.

I floated outside my body, looking down it. You haven't lived until you've seen your dead body beneath you. My eyes were stuck open as I lay in a ballooning pool of blood under my stomach. The sight should have made me sick to my stomach, but in fairness, it's not like I had a stomach anymore. I regarded the fact that I was dead as an interesting fact. That's how the dead's minds work.

The rooftop of the casino was a dim scene of blurry, twinkling bokeh—the city beyond the roof went on about its business because the world never stops turning when you die. The cars keep on keepin' on down the road, the clouds keep on a-scudding across the sky, and the only thing that stops is you. Dying at night is even more humbling; eventually, you realize that very soon, the sun will rise without you. The birds will take to the sky, the trees will keep swaying, and the world will keep on livin,' like my grandmama used to say.

An echoey bark tore me from my thoughts. Hazel's soul floated over to mine. It was the hazy essence of a dog, but it didn't look anything like her. Oh—that's another thing I forgot to tell you about—if you die with someone, they join you on the short journey to the afterlife. As for me, I died with my sweet pea. My heart stung for her death, but I'd have some good company in the great beyond.

Another voice floated up to me.

"Boss man, ain't this a bitch?"

Bo's soul floated next to me—gray, wavy, with a golden core. It was exactly how I saw him when I first encountered his soul in the spirit world.

I hovered over my body and swirled around it. Hazel followed me.

A reaper appeared on the other end of the pool. It was

Atwood. Even though I couldn't see his face, I knew his red tie. A gold rectangle flashed in his hand—an hourglass.

"Didn't think this day would come," Atwood said.

"I did," I said. "Generally speaking, of course."

Atwood held out his hand, and I readied myself for the come hither. Instead, he pointed behind me.

Fiona stood, her knife dripping with my blood.

"Wait right there, reaper," she said. "They're not going anywhere."

Atwood sprang an hourglass into his palm without replying.

Fiona tilted her head at my spirit. "Lester, you insisted on no innocent people dying. So you're going to get what you ask for. Ooooh, this is going to be soooo interesting!"

She pointed the bloody knife at Natkaal. The grasshopper demon screamed as he lifted into the air. Blue, viscous blood poured from his amputated leg and formed a string that circled the rooftop before floating to a stop over my body.

"You can thank me later," Fiona said.

The blue blood slammed into my stomach. My soul slid down into my body like someone was guiding it with a pulley.

Hazel barked at me, her golden core fading. Her soul drifted into its body too via the bite mark on her neck.

My vision flashed white amid Natkaal's excruciating screams.

I opened my eyes. My human eyes.

I lay next to the pool, but all my pain was gone. Just like in death.

I sat up. My death vision was gone. The world blasted back to full color and I didn't quite believe it at first. But the colors settled in, the wind blew, and Fiona's laughter rang in my ears.

Across the pool, Atwood collapsed his hourglass into his palm. Five souls floated next to him, electric blue lines pulsing around them. "See you again soon, Lester."

He disappeared, taking the souls with him in a flash.

Ant'ny and Harris were next to a cabana. Ant'ny was helping Harris up. Harris looked like he had been punched in the face.

Bo, Hazel, and I were sitting next to each other.

Fiona stood a few feet away from me, still holding the knife with my blood. She dropped it, and it clanged to the ground with a loud ring.

"We'll see each other again," she said. She took her beret and tossed it into the air as if she were at a college graduation. Long brown hair tumbled down to her shoulders. She ripped off her giant sunglasses, exposing her blood-veined eyes.

"Here we go!"

Balfouriel took her with its demon hands and carried her high into the air. She spread her hands in an embrace, like she was going to hug the sky.

"I win," she said as lightning struck her body, turning her to dust. The demon gathered her ashes in its human hands and ascended into the sky where a storm cloud was forming out of nowhere. It twinkled away as the cloud opened up rain on the rooftop.

I stared after her as the rain began to pour.

"Everyone all right?" I asked.

Then my eyes fell on the battered husks of the five hotel employees who had been sacrificed. I looked away and wept. My tears mixed in with the rain at the thought of these people gone from this earth for no reason other than a sociopathic woman's arrogance.

Bo put a hand on my shoulder. "It's not your fault, boss man."

I wiped away my tears and gazed upon what was left of the rooftop. This place had been one hell of a battlefield. Dead bats bobbing in the pool, remnants of magic circles on the concrete, ripped cabanas, and dead bodies.

"She turned to dust," Bo said. "Did that butterfly demon betray her?"

"She didn't die," Ant'ny said, scanning the sky.

"Her final shadow deal was complete," a strained voice said.

Natkaal lay next to one of the cabanas. His leg still bled profusely. Demons had a lot of blood, and Natkaal must have been able to spare enough to donate to me and Hazel and live to tell about it.

"We have just seen a wonder of the supernatural world," the grasshopper demon said, eyes sad. He pointed one of his destroyed wings at me. "We will talk about this day for centuries to come. And she connected us, necromancer."

The demon growled. "My blood now courses through your veins. It is distasteful to have saved your life."

"The disdain is mutual," I said, "but you started this."

Natkaal puffed. "Perhaps. But if I killed you now, I would kill a part of myself. We'll agree to end this night with a clean slate."

The demon stumbled to one foot.

"I'll take that deal," I said. "There's no reason to be enemies anymore."

Natkaal stared at Ant'ny with a scrutinizing gaze. "I suppose I should cure your third eye."

A wave of white energy surged through Ant'ny. He ran his hands over his face and sighed with relief. Harris patted him on the back, giving him some words of encouragement.

"Good luck to you, necromancer," Natkaal said. And in a blink, he was gone.

At least I scored one victory tonight.

"Boss man," Bo said, jamming a thumb at the hotel door.

Several armed guards walked onto the rooftop. They wore sunglasses and had broad chests.

"Excuse us," one of the guards said.

Harris flashed his badge. "Official business."

"Official, my ass," the guard said. "You're trespassing. I need all of you to come with us immediately."

"You're interfering with police business," Harris said, raising his voice.

"We won't tell you again," the guard said. He put his hands on his hips, signaling that he wasn't afraid to use his gun.

I motioned to Harris. "Let's go. It's not worth it."

The guards accompanied us into the hallway with the flesh-colored walls, into the elevator, across the hotel atrium, and toward the door.

As they escorted us out, a sign by the hotel's front desk caught my eye.

THANK YOU FOR COMING!

EFFECTIVE IMMEDIATELY, THE CASINO & HOTEL IS UNDER NEW MANAGEMENT. PARDON OUR DUST!

YOURS TRULY,

—F

My Lincoln Town Car was waiting for us under the porte-cochere. Someone had moved it, even though they didn't have the keys. Two sullen-faced valets opened the doors for us.

"This is your warning to stay off the premises," the guard said. "You've been blacklisted, and if you return, you will be killed. Have a nice night."

We looked at each other reluctantly as we got into my car and the guards politely shut the door for us. One of the guards motioned for us to follow him down the path out of the porte-cochere, through the parking lot, and onto the street adjacent to the hotel. Bo followed him slowly.

Bo turned out of the parking lot and swung the car right on the next street so we passed parallel to the hotel. In the rain, the building's neon frame pulsed many colors brightly in rapid succession.

My heart skipped a beat when I saw the name in neon

letters along the side of the building: THE FIONA CASINO. Above the hotel, stark white letters said HOTEL FIONA.

"She did it," I said quietly.

"Did what?" Ant'ny asked.

"She cured her vampirism," I said as rain barreled down on the windshield. "We lost."

CHAPTER THIRTY-ONE

They say it's good to be humbled from time to time because it builds character. It's true on the schoolyard; talk trash a little too much and you'll eventually get a right hook to the face, which will make you think twice about it next time. It's true as a parent; one day, your kid will adopt one of your bad habits and you'll realize just how flimsy the "do as I say, not as I do" argument truly is.

It's also true in necromancy.

I fought against valiant foes in the Vampire Collective and Fiona. I fought them with every skill I knew how to use, and I still laid myself into the bitter jaws of defeat. Fiona broke me like a nutcracker.

Like I said, humility.

As we parked in my garage, I was just glad this was all over.

"I can't thank you enough," Harris said as we got out of the car. "I wish it would have turned out differently, but we made a pretty good team."

"I guess you could say that," I said, shaking his hand. The detective was just as bruised and battered as me. We both needed a long, hot shower.

"I owe you," Harris said. "I imagine this won't be the last time we work together."

I remembered Joyner.

"Do you know anyone at city hall that might be able to help a friend?" I asked. I told him about Joyner's electrical and water woes. Harris listened, thinking. He told me he'd see what he can do.

And then Detective Damian Harris said goodbye and walked into the rain, down my gravel alley to a black sedan that was waiting for him at the corner. He got in, and it sped away.

"Hallelujah, Hallelujah, Hallelujah," Bo said. "Now I can take a nap."

"And while you do, I'm putting the phone off the hook," I said, opening the door to my backyard. The pop-up thunderstorm was still raging, sending needle-like sheets of rain into my yard.

Ant'ny unrolled his black bandanna and gave it to me with the medical pouch Joyner had made for him. The pouch was light in my hands, and the ingredients were a brownish-yellow soup. "Tell Joyner I said thanks."

I took the bandanna, but Ant'ny didn't let it go.

"I still don't know what to think about all this, dawg," he said.

"I won't blame you if you never want to talk to me again," I said.

"Come on, man," Ant'ny said. "I don't abandon my friends like that."

I sighed and gave a tired grin. Knowing that I still had Ant'ny's friendship was a relief.

"Your secret's safe with me," Ant'ny said. "If you gotta pick me up from work and you're embroiled in some supernatural stuff—maybe tell me to take a taxi. I can take a hint."

"Deal," I said.

Ant'ny gave Bo a fist bump.

"Ant Man, you up for cards tomorrow?" Bo asked.

"Always," Ant'ny said. "Too bad I couldn't thrash you tonight."

Bo shook a finger at Ant'ny. "Everybody knows I would have rolled you up and smoked ya, bruh. Just you wait."

He flipped up his hoodie, ran through the needling rain into my gangway, let himself out my front gate, and was gone.

I held the bandanna. It was still stained with demon blood. I'd have to burn it in my fireplace tonight.

The same bloodstain on this bandanna was running through my veins now. What did it mean? I had a feeling it wouldn't take long to find out.

"Welp, that's another adventure behind us, boss man," Bo said.

"We're alive to talk about it, so that's okay with me," I said.

"Want some tea?" he asked.

I fingered the bandanna. "There's somewhere I want to go. Just you and me."

"Dinner?" Bo asked, confused.

I shook my head and got in the car.

∼

There aren't too many Grimsbys in the white pages. I found them pretty easily. I remembered Fiona's parents' names from the missing person poster she showed me. They lived in a neighborhood in St. Charles, about twenty minutes away.

I could tell you about the neighborhood of St. Charles, but honestly, I wasn't thinking about my surroundings too much as Bo drove the car and Hazel took a nap in the backseat. I-70 blazed by as I thought about the night.

Fiona did exactly what she said she was going to do: she cured her vampirism and switched her need to feed on blood with offerings from the public. The Fiona Casino and Hotel would be so successful that the steady stream of money and attention in one weekend was probably enough to feed her forever.

And as a bonus, if Fiona was true to her word, there were no more vampires in the world. She killed them all. Every last one. Trust me when I say that I didn't exactly feel sorry for the bloodsuckers.

If all of this was true, there was something else I had to see for myself.

Bo turned off the highway. A few intersections later, he cruised through a residential neighborhood.

"There," I said, pointing at a white house with black shutters. This was the first time I saw it from the front, but there was no mistaking it.

There was a blue hatchback parked in the driveway.

Bo looked at me. "Round two?"

I shook my head and told him to park on the curb in front of the house. We waited as the rain crashed down on the car in ragged sheets.

The curtains were open. Fiona's mother moved through the living room and passed a curio resting against the wall. I recognized her from earlier. She looked like Fiona, but older. The house was warmly decorated, the kind of place you called home. Some folks' houses looked like museums; Fiona's parents seemed like average, everyday people to me.

Her mother was setting a dining room table. Three spots.

Fiona's dad, a skinny middle-aged man with black hair and wearing a polo, brought several plates of steaming steak to the table. He set the plates down, brushed off his trousers, and gestured his hands for a hug.

Someone drifted out of the living room into the dining room, into his arms. My heart raced at the sight of long brown hair, maroon pants, and leather boots.

Fiona hugged her father as if she were making up for lost time. He rubbed her back and held her. Then he released her reluctantly, as if he would lose her if he let go. He disappeared into the kitchen.

Fiona must have known we were watching because she sauntered over to the window and stood there, watching us in the rain.

She smiled, but this time with all human teeth. The same youthful smile I'd seen in her missing person poster. No fangs. Instead of blood-veined eyes, she watched us with beautiful chestnut brown eyes.

She waved, her mouth curving into an arrogant smirk. Bo and I didn't return the gesture.

Then, Fiona grabbed the window curtains and closed them. I'll never forget the flash of evil in her eyes just before the curtains covered her face.

"Whoa," Bo said.

The house shook as giant orange and black butterfly wings rose from the roof.

The wings clicked like a socket wrench in the rain as they expanded and folded over the entire house. The place swirled away in a quiet twister, replaced by a park with a children's playground and a sandbox.

"She wiped out the entire vampire race just to be reunited with her family, huh?" Bo asked. "Now I've seen everything."

"We'll never see everything," I said, motioning him to drive.

As Bo pulled away, I gave a final glance at the newly created rain-drenched park. Fiona *wanted* me to see her. Wanted me to see her new life begin. She had known all along that I would come.

I still stand by what I said: I don't care how many shadow deals she did and how skilled she *thought* she was. One day, the demons would betray her and shatter her perfect new life. The demons always got you in the end. Always. I didn't want to be around when that moment came—that kind of suffering is best done alone.

But her voice kept running through my head like poison. What if she never paid any consequences?

What if there was a threshold in life where you could be so evil that it just flat out didn't matter anymore? That you could purify evil with evil itself?

I turned on my cassette player and rested my head against my fist, lost in thought as moody jazz filled the car.

For now, I had my life. And my sweet pea, Hazel. Bo and I would live to have another adventure. That was something to be grateful for.

If Fiona and I ever met again, I wanted to know who would be right.

THE END.

GET BOOK 3

Lester's adventures continue in Book 3, *Spirit Chaser.*
Grab your copy today at www.michaellaronn.com/spiritchaser.

MEET MICHAEL LA RONN

Michael La Ronn has written many books of science fiction & fantasy. Michael was born and raised in St. Louis, Missouri where *The Good Necromancer* series takes place.

In 2012, a life-threatening illness made him realize that storytelling was his #1 passion. He's devoted his life to writing ever since, making up whatever story makes him fall out of his chair laughing the hardest. Every day.

To get updates when he releases new work + other bonuses, sign up by visiting www.michaellaronn.com/fanclub.